William the Conqueror
vs
King Harold

William the Conqueror
vs

King Harold

Jesse Lee Vint

Copyright © by Jesse Vint III
LCCN: 2015900578
ISBN 10; 1507524137
ISBN 13: 9781507524138
Credits: Edited by Carolyne Cathey; cover painted by May
Lee; graphics by by Jerod McKnight; cover design by JLV3;
RESEARCH: WIKIPEDIA; LOS ANGELES PUBLIC LIBRARY;
INTERNET
Wolf's Eye Publishing
CreateSpace Independent Publishing Platform
North Charleston, South Carolina

From the pages of: *William the Conqueror vs King Harold*

--- "It's all very clear to me now," began William. "You, my good man, are no longer in the province of Henry's Paris, where a well-known nest of perfumed, dandified fops are known to flourish, and have become as thick as mosquitoes in a late-night swamp. You are now in Normandy, land of the north man, and you are assured of challenges here." *William the Conqueror's words to the Green Knight*

--- Harold bent down and picked up Big John's helmet and gave it a vigorous shake. Big John's head fell out and hit the sand. With his left hand he reached down and lifted up Big John's head by his hair and held his face nose to nose with his own before asking this question: "Where be your jibes now, Big John, Cleaver of Men? Are you still amused?"

---"So be it! Then old Hardrada shall once again leave many bones behind to glut the ravenous birds of this fair land as the Anglish shall soon feel the might of the Hammer of Thor!" ---*The words of King Hardrada of Norway to King Harold of Angle Land; the Battle of Stamford Bridge*

---"I am a Scot, with the blood of the Highlander. We Scots grew out of the ground, exactly like the trees, the grass, the flowers, and the wildlife; and like the rivers and streams, our blood has coursed down the mountains and through the valleys since the beginning of time. I love the cold, the mist, the ancient megaliths, the bag pipes, the songs, the poetry, and the most beautiful faces of any people that god has ever put on this earth. But most of all I miss my son...little Malory." -- *The words of the Green Knight to Harold and Adelize*

--- Harold thrust his broadsword toward William's mid-section. William turned and moved only the necessary one inch as the silver blade flashed past, and then countered to the crown of Harold's helmet with the mace, which knocked Harold back. Harold seemed dazed, but it was only a ruse. William threw a lateral right.

Harold ducked, pivoted on his left foot, and suddenly Harold was no longer in front of William – he was behind him! William had never in his life seen this move, which he later described as "faster than a falcon's dive".

--- A moment later Harold heard the snort of a horse and turned to see, emerging from the dense fog, Spanish Dancer slowly, very slowly, galloping past with the naked witch on his back. She screamed out as she passed Harold, "*September victory, October defeat, Harold's reign, six luckless feet.*"

---Adelize sat down on a bench and tossed her lengthy blonde hair out of her eyes. She crossed her long lean legs while smiling up at Harold. The moonlight lit her deep blue green eyes, and accentuated the pout of her lips. She gave Harold a serious look, and then tossed it away with a full laugh that echoed off the castle walls and spilled out into the courtyard. She patted the seat next to her while smiling. "Please sit next to me," and after a moment she placed her hand on his forehead. "Your forehead is damp, and your hand is still trembling. What kind of farewell party was that, that would daunt my dauntless knight?"

---The pain in Konan the Great's eyes vanished, and was replaced by a deep respect for this mysterious knight who traveled the lands of Europe without a name. "Please know that you will always have a home in Brittany, Green Knight." The entire conversation between the two had taken place in Gaelic.

---"Who might you be, good sir?" asked Geoffrey the Hammer.
"I am only a weary traveler who has come from the hot burning sands of hell to bring you the news of your death, good sir. I am avenging the death of my brother, the Green Knight."
"Your challenge is joyfully accepted, Black Knight, but before I kill you, please tell me your hidden name so that when I wear your skull on my belt and show it to my children's children, it will have a name for them to play with, along with your hairless skull."
"Very well," said the Black Knight. "I am Harold, King of the Anglish."

--- It was autumn in Normandy, and the afternoon was sunny, quiet, and uncharacteristically warm. The shadows were long in the middle of the day, and the trees, most of them, were already bare. Mother Nature looked as though she were laying down for her winter rest, but somehow found that she was unable to fall asleep, so she simply laid there and allowed the remaining warmth of the season to slowly sedate her until autumn gradually faded away.

---"Because I have, in my long life, dear Lord, seen too many times when darkness prevailed over light – and when wrong prevailed over right – and it is because of this that we are hoping and praying that the great fiery light of 1066 that streaked across the sky earlier this year and passed over this blessed land of ours was none other than your holy messenger known to us as "Winged Victory" and that this was your sign to us that she would be standing with us on the field during the great battle tomorrow, and to see that the Anglish Dragon defeats forever the Lion of Normandy! That is our prayer, dear Lord. Amen!" *The Anglish prayer prior to the Battle of Hastings, led by Verser the Varangian.*

--- William remembered that he had placed both his hands under her chin, tilted her face up, and putting the tip of his nose to hers quietly said, "Don't you worry, my beautiful princess Adelize. You know who I am by now, and I will protect your handsome king. And just know that in an odd way, Adelize, I haven't given up on the idea that we will all be a family of one someday."

A word from the author:

What appeared to be a mighty mass of flame, now known as Halley's Comet, made its rare appearance and blazed across the western sky in the year 1066. Even rarer than Halley's Comet was the appearance of three warrior kings on this same year in North West Europe. All three of these warrior-kings felt that they had a claim to the British crown, and all three were known for never taking a step backward. For this reason 1066 was a year unlike any other in Western history.

William the Conqueror is one of the most dashing, powerful, and massively influential figures in all of world history. Equally fascinating, I believe, is Harold Godwinson, crowned King Harold II of Angle Land (England) in January of 1066. Haarald (Hard Rule) Hardrada, the Viking warrior/king of Norway, was also a colorful figure who played a major role in the destiny of world history in 1066. Hardly anybody, including college graduates, knows anything about any of these extraordinary men.

Why is this? Frankly, I don't have a clue.

My goal is to change that. To make what is *almost always a historical dry read* as exciting and interesting as possible I incorporated an "Arthurian" feel to the material. To describe exactly what that is I will turn to one of Britain's greatest, William Caxton. Here is a paragraph out of Caxton's words when he introduced Sir Thomas Malory's monumental classic" Le Morte d'Arthur" (The Death of Arthur) to Europe in the year 1485:

"Wherin they shalle fynde many Ioyous and playsaunt hystoryes / and noble & renomed actes of humanyte / gentylnesse and chyualryes / For herein may be seen noble chyualrye / Curtosye / Humanyte / frendlynesse / hardynesse / loue / frendshyp / Cowardyse / Murdre / hate / vertue / and synne / Doo after the good and leue the euyl / and it shal brynge you to good fame and renommee / And for to passe the tyme thys boook shal be plesaunte to rede in / but for to gyue fayth and byleue that al is trewe that is conteyned herin / ye be at your lyberte / but al is wryton for our doctryne / and for to beware that we falle not to vyce ne synne / but texersyse and folowe vertu / by whyche we may come and atteyne to good fame and renomme in thys lyf / and after thys shorte and transytorye lyf to come vnto euerlastyng blysse in heuen / the whyche he graunte vs that reygneth in heuen the blessyd Trynyte Amen."

I have boundless admiration for William Caxton's words, and aspired for all I am worth and stand for in this life to do the same with this book about William, Harold, and Adelize. To do this I took the skeleton of historical events of that time and then fleshed it out by "Arthurizing" them, so that the reader would hopefully be entertained, and perhaps even inspired to do further research on these great people and their extraordinary times.

Of course William the Conqueror is only a subject matter – until you find the story – which is always a writer's greatest challenge. It was a lot of hard work, but there is a story here, and I believe it to be a very good one. After heavily researching this subject for close to a year in library cellars that had guards standing over me while reading rare books I came out of my sleep at three in the morning and said, "That's it! That's the story! I believe that the essence of this book is a really unique story that has never been told, either in print or in film.

This is not easy to talk about, but it's even harder to stay quiet: I am also hopeful that my work is not stolen from me, as "Back to the Future" was {formerly "Fathers and Sons" at the time I was writing it. Go to youtube for the thirty minute details of that literary theft} If it is stolen, this time I will not hesitate to march the no-integrity no-class lying thieving moral degenerates into an empty cement mixer and drive around town with the mixer rotating while the black-hearted squealing moral degenerates bang around on the inside – and in the meantime I will play "I'm Singing in the Rain" on a CD at a very high volume, and I will love every minute of it.

Anyway, after reading this book the reader will know a little more about a fascinating period in European history that they perhaps didn't know about before, and hopefully have a good time while learning about this amazing era, its extraordinary people, and the sacrifices that were made in the building of a great nation, formerly known as Angle Land.

Respectfully,

Jesse Lee Vint III

Table of Contents

Chapter I: The Shipwreck of Harold Godwinson 1

Chapter II: The Duke of Normandy 7

Chapter III: William, Harold, and Count Guy 22

Chapter IV: Harold meets Adelize and Matilda 29

Chapter V: The Green Knight 45

Chapter VI: Matilda and Spanish Dancer 49

Chapter VII: Konan the Great and the Fearless Tower 59

Chapter VIII: The Black Knight 72

Chapter IX: Tostig; the Diving Duck 83

Chapter X: Adelize, Harold, and the Green Knight 89

Chapter XI: The Duke and the Earl; an Interesting
Proposal 99

Chapter XII: The Covenant over Bones of Saints 104

Chapter XIII: Princess Adelize and her
Dauntless Knight 110

Chapter XIV: The Return of Harold 117

Chapter XV: Edward the Confessor; King Maker 129

Chapter XVI: The Royal Banquet 141

Chapter XVII: A Witch's Prophesy 147

Chapter XVIII: The Prophesy of Starlings 169

Chapter XIX: Tostig and William 176

Chapter XX: Two Very Different Meetings 183

Chapter XXI: The Holiness of a South Wind 188

Chapter XXII: Tostig and Hardrada 193

Chapter XXIII: The Invasion of York 196

Chapter XXIV: King Harold Marches to York 201

Chapter XXV: St. Valery 209

Chapter XXVI: The Battle of Stamford Bridge 218

Chapter XXVII: William and Adelize:
Their Sacred Promises 233

Chapter XXVIII: The Nordic Omen 242

Chapter XXIX: London learns of the Norman Landing ... 245

Chapter XXX: Verser the Varangian 255

Chapter XXXI: The Battle of Hastings 269

Chapter XXXII: The Wonderful Ghosts of
Waltham Abbey 305

About the author: Jesse Lee Vint III was born and raised in Tulsa. While at Oklahoma University he decided that the film business is where he should be, so he left to study acting. After over a hundred films and television shows he moved to Portland, Oregon – where he currently lives. Some of the characters he played were gunfighters during the Wild West era, such as "Tulsa Jack" and "Charlie Springer" – both of these were starring parts in films with James Garner. He played the outlaw "Bob Dalton" in the television movie "Belle Starr; a lead role as "Amos Calendar", one of the original cowboys on the Goodnight trail in 1868 in Universal Studio's epic mini-series based on James Michener's classic novel, "Centennial". Other cinematic cowboys were "Slick Callahan" in "Bobby Jo and The Outlaw" – a film that he starred in with Lynda Carter that was released worldwide; "Jingo Johnson", a modern day cowboy in the film "Black Oak Conspiracy" that was released worldwide; he was the Busch Beer cowboy in a commercial that ran nationally for eight years called, "Lone Cowboy"; as "Tex" in a "Matlock", and as "Al 'Cowboy' Roberts" in twenty-five episodes of "One Life to Live". He was the gunman known as "Turk" in the television series "Hart to Hart". He also starred as "Insane Wayne", the mercenary who tried to take out the "A-Team". The name of the episode was "Insane Wayne". Jesse worked with Sam Elliot and Cybil Shepherd on the western show, "Yellow Rose" as Matt Colby, the ranch hand; and as the rodeo cowboy "Tibby Tucker" in "The Incredible Hulk". He played the outlaw, "Toby Harris" on a "Bonanza", and the rancher "Tom Carson" in an episode of "Grimm", and the Texas cattle rancher "Tommy Tacker" in the movie "Bug".

He starred as the outlaw "Cody Pierce" on a special two part episode of the television series, "Young Guns" filmed in Tucson. He played a trouble-shooting space cowboy twice, in futuristic films. The first was as "Andy Wolf" in the classic film "Silent Running", and the second was as "Matt Colby" in "Forbidden World". Both of these films played worldwide, and are still playing worldwide. Jesse Vint played one of the major characters in the epic film "Little Big Man" with Dustin Hoffman -- about 'Custer's last stand', a film that he worked on for six months. He also played principal parts in the film classics, "Chinatown", and "Earthquake." Jesse starred in the film, MACON COUNTY LINE, which broke box office records all over America and internationally as well. He won the World Celebrity Chess Tournament held at the Century Plaza in Los Angeles in 1988 and is still the reigning champion. Jesse votes on and attends the Academy Awards and the Emmy's every year.

Dedicated to

Harold, Adelize,

and the

Green Knight

Note: Not that it matters, but much of this is straight out of the history books; the rest is straight out of my head.

CHAPTER I

The Shipwreck of Harold Godwinson

Ghostly forms in the mist stalked the ship as though it were a harpooned whale that had fatally resigned and was now being driven toward the beach by incessant waves. An earlier storm had ripped many of the sails of the Anglish ship to shreds. Some of those sails were connected to heavy timber which had crashed violently into the deck, not only partially destroying the function of the ship, but several lives of its crew members. The ship was in trouble. The light of a three quarter moon was diffused by the heavy fog and so the visibility was severely limited; the captain and the crew members could only rely on the sound of waves breaking against the rocks and surf for navigation.

The search was for a quiet bay that they could anchor in, gather food and water, tend to the wounded, and make the necessary repairs. There were light-houses along this part of the Norman Coast of north-west France put there by the descendants of the Norse man, or "Normans" as they were now called. These lighthouses would serve to guide them to safety, if they could only sight one.

Finally, the long-awaited shout to the captain from a crew member positioned near the bow,

"Ahoy! Lights to the starboard, Captain!"

A cheer went up from the crew. The captain felt all anxiety melt away. He dropped his chin to his chest and said quietly, "Thank the almighty God in heaven." He crossed himself and blotted the excess moisture from his eyes with the sleeve of his coat. The captain nodded to a seaman and the trusted sailor took the helm as the captain made his way toward the bow to take a look.

Emerging from the fog and joining the captain at his side was a tall, well-proportioned man that appeared to be in his mid-thirties. The man was Harold Godwinson, the Earl of Essex, who was sometimes described by his contemporaries as a carouser, a jouster, a fighter, and a wenchifier. Harold advised the captain to use caution, but he was interrupted by the captain before he could finish:

"I know…I know…I know…" said the captain, signaling his impatience before continuing, "The false lights ruse – which are false lights put up by unscrupulous scavengers--for the purpose of tricking mariners into crashing into the reef and looting wreckage. Your father and I sailed this coast many times, so I know all about it. That's why I'm the captain of this ship, and you are only an Earl," said the captain, laughing good-naturedly.

"Now, my boy, the reason I know that these particular lights aren't false... here, please allow the old captain to tell you a little trick, Harold, on how to distinguish the real from the false ones --"

The captain was pointing to the position of the lights relative to the thundering of the surf on the shore, when there came a heavy crash as the ship slammed into a submerged rock. The captain, Harold, and the crew members were hurled violently toward the bow. All was pandemonium as water gushed across the deck. In seconds the ship tilted, masts snapped, ropes broke, cargo slid across the deck, and above the booming thunder of tons of lumber snapping and breaking were the terrified cries of people that knew that they were getting their final glimpse of light.

The barely distinguishable forms on the Normandy shore leaped and shouted with joy at the mariner's misfortune. Business had been slow for the scavengers, and to them the loud crash of the Anglish ship against the rocks was a glorious sound unlike any other. They hugged and congratulated one another as they waited for the cargo and bodies to wash ashore; which were seen by them as gifts from their god, who they thanked over and over while on their knees in the sand with tears of gratitude flowing down their cheeks.

The following morning, although it was barely light and the fog was still heavy, figures moved through the wreckage, most of which was still moving to and fro with the surf. Two of the scavengers fought over a bottle, another put on a seaman's hat and was chased across the sand by others trying to snatch it away from him; and two more raced toward a small barrel, reaching it at the same time. They rolled in the sand while tearing at one another's ears and nose, until the ownership of the barrel was finally decided.

Things continued in this vein until one of them saw a body draped across a mast that had washed ashore. They cautiously approached the body of Harold Godwinson, and then hunkered down to observe it. After a moment one of them started to take off Harold's boots, but he was stopped by another, who observed that the man was no ordinary sailor – and better yet, he was still breathing. This gave them an idea. They dragged him to a dry area of the sandy beach and covered him with portions of canvas from the sails that they had gathered from the flotsam and jetsam.

After much arguing, bickering, and shoving they finally decided on a runner and sent him along. Before he left the runner was told that if he defected then his child would be fed to the sea creatures. The long legged runner said that this was something that he already knew and set off on his journey.

Later that morning most of the fog had lifted. The scavengers sighted two distant riders moving toward them at an easy lope. Even though they were still far away, because of their flying capes, they were easily identified as noblemen.

The scavengers waved to the noblemen and beckoned them to follow them. The noblemen dismounted and handed the reins of their horses to one of the men without looking at him, and followed the scavengers down the path to the sandy shore. One of the noblemen, Count Guy, approached Harold, squatted down, perused him from head to foot, put his ear on the Earl's heart and listened, and then stood up. He turned to the scavengers and held out his hand with his palm skyward.

"Who has the ring?" After a moment he said, "One more time....who has the ring?" The count had noticed a bleached area on Harold's finger, where a ring had just recently been removed.

After a moment a man stepped forward and handed Count Guy the ring. The man, with a terrified tremor in his voice, apologized profusely, but Count Guy waved him away while never taking his eyes off the ring.

The signet of royalty was easily recognized. He nodded while turning the ring over and over, allowing the sun to light the dark crevices of the crafted silver and gold. After a moment he looked up at the man who had handed him the ring and said,

"Well, you are right for a change! He is an Anglish nobleman, and he will, without a doubt, bring a hefty ransom. You did well!" He tossed some coins on the ground, and after the scavengers had fought over them he had them build a crude cot for the Anglish Earl, utilizing the wreckage from the ship -- a cot that could easily transport the Earl the short distance to Count Guy's manor, where Harold's health was to be restored in full.

CHAPTER II

The Duke of Normandy

WILLIAM, THE DUKE OF NORMANDY, was descended from the 'wolves of the sea' as they were sometimes known; others simply knew them as "The Vikings". The Vikings had settled in northwest France beginning in 906 a.d., when Rolf the Granger and his clan landed there from Norway. They named it "Land of the North People", or simply, "Normandy". The year was now 1065. William was a sixth generation direct descendant of Rolf. Like his ancestors he was a tall, fair-haired, Viking with blue eyes and a slender build. When these Vikings stepped onto the land, there was nothing there; but Normandy, within a short period of time, had become a showpiece for architecture, roads, towns, a quality of life, and a military second to none in coastal Europe.

While growing up, William was a child without a childhood. In his youth he lived under the continuous threat of either being kidnapped and held for ransom, or killed. This threat usually came from relatives.

Every time a descendent of Rolf the Granger died, there were arguments and bickering over the inheritance of these vast estates; arguments that were often settled by force. Because of this there was a continuous turbulence in the lives of those who had been blessed with Rolf's blood. William as a child, they say, never slept in any one place for any length of time. By the time he was in his late teens he trusted very few, and he had learned that ultimately force was the solution to any problem.

A neighboring province just to the east of the Duke's territory, Mantes, proved to be an irritant to the Duke. The Governor of Mantes was known to have more than once sent hunting parties into Normandy. When asked about this trespassing, he would remind the Duke's envoys that he, the Governor, was a popular man, and that he had many friends and allies in the region, and that his French blood went back to the beginning of time, and that they were losing patience with these Norwegian newcomers, and especially The Duke.

"The Norwegians are only guests in this part of the world, and they should mind their manners," he was known to have said. It was only a matter of time until The Duke, who had been fighting in the field since he was nineteen, paid the Governor of Mantes a royal visit. The Governor was confident that such a visit was inevitable, but he was also confident that the hierarchy from the neighboring provinces would unite with him to drive this war-monger away, as they always promised they would do since their feelings about The Duke were identical to his own.

He was wrong. Now Mantes was under siege by William, and the neighbors in the nearby provinces had propped their feet up in front of their fireplaces and stayed home.

William, his helmet visor up and wearing his shining silver armor, dropped his hand as a signal. A siege machine hurled a large stone to the top of the castle wall. It knocked a chunk off the top, but the castle still seemed to be in good defensive order. William gave the signal to light the firebrand, and the siege machine hurled a ball of fire to the top of the castle; the fire was quickly extinguished, however. William stepped forward, and perhaps prematurely, demanded their surrender.

"Why postpone your fate, Governor? We are here to stay, and we will continue pounding your walls by day and by night – our soldiers eating well and sleeping well – until we either knock your gates down, or wait for you to throw them open yourselves out of thirst and famine."

William paused, carefully allowing his words to take hold before escalating the tension.

"But I'm warning you, Governor, if you make us wait until that time then I have promised my men that they may reward themselves with your daughters, your sisters, and your mothers -- and for our entertainment your sons, your brothers, and your fathers will be thrown from the top of the wall while you look on. Your seed shall be transformed into Norman seed for all eternity, and Mantes will lie buried beneath its ashes. Well what say you now, Governor, and how much do you love your people? My patience has ended, and I demand an answer!"

There was no appearance from the Governor. Instead several soldiers, who were confident in the castle's defensive structure, began shouting obscenities. One of the soldiers, from the top of the castle wall, bent over and exhibited his buttocks while yelling something about "William the Bastard". The soldier, in further defiance, ran across the top of the castle wall, and from time to time he would bend over and drop his pants. Soon the Mantes soldiers were convinced that their defensive position was impenetrable, for if there was any way at all that the Normans could have attacked them, they certainly would have done so after this crass exhibition by one of their own.

Incensed, William stepped forward and removed his helmet; his golden hair flashed in the sun. The soldiers at the top of the castle wall suddenly became quiet; they were having a first-look at the Duke of Normandy, whose name they had heard several times a day since they could remember – and now here he was, brazen as could be, and so far he was in every way consistent with all the tales that they had heard about him. After a moment William raised his sword high over his head and began to speak, and he spoke with the ease, the calm, and the authority of one who had never lost a battle in his life:

"Tell me Governor, do you have a knight, just one knight, your very best knight, that wishes to decide this by single combat. Send this knight to challenge me. If he wins, we leave. If I win, throw open your gates and be done with it."

This challenge was entirely unexpected and fostered several highly intense exchanges among the cadre of Mantes. William waited patiently. He knew, in order for the province of Mantes to avoid an everlasting humiliation that they had to have at least one person among them who would accept the Duke's challenge; how else could they live with themselves if they didn't?

The Governor, who had been watching everything from a position of hiding, now stepped forward. Perhaps to show William and his men that he was also a man of courage he stood on top of a ledge on the summit of the castle wall without hanging on to support of any kind, but only looking straight down at William.

His long auburn-streaked grey hair and grey beard shined brightly in the late morning sun. With his deep purple robe flowing in the wind, and after nodding profoundly for what seemed to be on both sides a very long time, he replied:

"We accept your challenge, William, and we send our champion to meet you. He is the trainer of our soldiers. We trust that God is on his side, since all of France knows that you, as son of the man known far and wide as, 'Robert the Devil', are the devil's spawn."

The gates were thrown open and a mounted knight with lance and shield galloped in a burning fury across the drawbridge, straight toward The Duke. William leveled his broadsword and pointed it directly at the charging knight. He stood steady as a rock as the charging knight, slowly lowering his lance, bore down on him. At the last second William stepped to the side, pivoted, and jammed the broadsword upward into the horse's chest. The front legs of the horse lost their use. It tumbled forward, throwing the knight over its head.

The knight bounced several times before coming to a stop. After a moment the knight stirred. With some effort he rose to his feet, his armor clanking and grinding.

The sergeant tossed William his mace. William caught the mace with his left; his right arm had been ripped open by the knight's lance, and now the blood flowed freely down the sleeve of his tunic.

The knight signaled that he wanted to remove some of his cumbersome gear. William nodded his assent. The knight, after removing some of his armor walked to his horse, which was already taking its last breath, and pulled a sword from a sheath. He turned to William and held up his sword, ready to defend himself. William, whose favorite weapon was known to be the mace, turned back to his opponent.

The knight pretended to make a couple of warm-up overhead swings, and then, in a surprise move, suddenly leaped toward William with a lateral slash toward William's neck. William barely moved his head and countered with a sharp rap of the mace to the side of the knight's helmet.

The knight staggered backward. Green flashes of light swirled before his eyes, and then cleared. "What happened?" he thought to himself. This time he slashed toward William's left knee. "If the knee were disabled, then the fight was won," was something his students had heard him say a hundred times; but this was William, and not one of his students. William took a short step back, and as the sword whistled past his knee he stepped in with a severe blow to the bridge of the knight's nose. The knight's head jerked back and blood spewed high into the air. Within seconds the knight's light blue tunic was blood red. The onlookers on top of the castle wall had grown quiet. To many the outcome was already certain.

The knight now realized that playing chess with William was not a viable strategy, so he screamed at the top of his lungs while slashing broadly and wildly, knowing that this would lead to either a quick victory or a quick death. To the knight either of these outcomes would be acceptable. What would never be acceptable was for him, the trainer of soldiers, to be humiliated any further.

William sidestepped, slipped, and parried all attempts, and then finally cracked the skull of the knight with his mace – a crack that was so loud that it flushed a covey of quail from a nearby field, and sent a chill down the spine of the onlookers from the upper rim of the castle. The knight was already soaring to Valhalla before he hit the ground.

William turned to the Governor and said, "Perhaps Governor, your challenger will do better in his next life."

After a quiet moment the Governor turned to his men and asked them to open the gates and allow William and his men to enter the castle, adding "May God have mercy on us."

William and his men, on the lookout for treachery, carefully formed their columns and marched through the gates of the Mantes castle. Once inside the Governor delivered the keys to William while William was still on horseback. The Governor turned to his men and announced,

"We now yield to William, Duke of Normandy our humble chateau', and our insignificant lives, hoping only that clemency—"

But William talked over him, saying "Now Governor, bring me the naked soldier that called me....the name."

All turned in the direction of the guilty soldier, who was hoping that his antics would be seen as somewhat humorous and forgotten. Once he realized that this was not going to be the case he began scampering along the gangplank around the upper rim of the castle. Several of the Norman archers saw this as an opportunity to sharpen their skills, and soon they were demonstrating their prowess to the Mantes soldiers, who stood by as the man provided the Normans with laughs while he dodged arrows. It was all first rate entertainment for the Norman knights. Eventually, though, the man caught a couple of arrows and a cold darkness entered his body. It was the guest that never left, and the man fell from the high rafters to his death.

In high spirits William addressed his soldiers, "Hungry men? Let's feast! The Governor is our host, and he has assured us that we, as his honored guests, will be greatly satisfied with tonight's table."

All let out a cheer. Soon barrels of ale were rolled out from the Governor's private cellar into the massive hall that was supported by precision cut stones and massive beams. There of course was the standard mead fermented from wildflower honey, but the Governor also had his own special ale. The ale, the Governor confided, was fermented from an unusual native oat and a wild red berry that was peculiar to the region. The soldiers, as they drank this extraordinary ale in the giant hall lit with torches, agreed that the Governor was not exaggerating; the ale was the finest that they had ever tasted. The salted venison and wild boar from the Governor's private locker from deep below the ground, where the temperature was always low, was being grilled in a fire area of huge stones just outside the great hall. Conquest, food, and drink! Life was good, and later in the night there would be encounters with some women that were no doubt hidden away by the men in secret passages somewhere.

The Governor, predictably, was now intent on becoming William's best friend; he personally poured the ale around the long table; he apologized over and over for having sent his archers into Normandy for venison and boar, and he hoped that all would be forgiven once he proved that he would be protective of Normandy's interests for life. He was willing to hand over his two daughters as hostages, knowing that they would be well taken care of, and knowing that they would also learn the ways of the Normans, and the peculiar language that had evolved in Normandy due to linguistic drift. The Governor respectfully described the tongue as Norman-French. He was corrected by William, who described it as Nordic-Gaelic. After a moment both agreed that they were probably saying the same thing, using different terms.

While William was eating and drinking with his left hand, his right arm was being tended to and wrapped by the Governor's special medical staff. There was a regular conference going on regarding his arm, which William seemed oblivious to as he listened to the Governor make one wild and meaningless promise after another while pouring his prized ale for William's cadre.

The soldiers from the other side began quietly inquiring to William's soldiers as to the possibility of riding with William, for William clearly was a man that knew how to take care of his soldiers. The soldiers felt that it was an honor to ride with the Duke of Normandy; it was one of the chief reasons for his great success. Another reason was that William himself was the ultimate soldier, and even his enemies, which he had no shortage of, said that no man ever sat a horse finer, or showed more courage and fighting skill than the Duke of Normandy.

The Governor's wolfhounds had adopted William, and refused to leave his side while William was at the table. Perhaps it had something to do with William allowing them to take a chair at the table with him and his knights, and feeding them large portions of boar meat instead of simply tossing them a bone now and then. William was commenting on the extraordinary size of the wolfhounds, which were larger than most men, when he was approached by a messenger with an obvious sense of urgency. William asked that the message be read aloud while he continued roughly playing with the wolfhounds.

"It says here" began the Sergeant, that, 'Harold, Earl of Essex from Angle Land, has survived a shipwreck and is being held by your cousin, Count Guy."

William snatched the message from the Sergeant and read it for himself, making sure that the Sergeant had not made a mistake. His men noted that he was becoming increasingly excited as he continued to read the message over and over to himself. Finally he looked up at his men, who were all wondering what on earth this could be about, and said to them,

"Harold, The Earl Of Essex! I remember Harold of Essex from my visit to the land of the Angles twelve years ago. They say that Harold's brother, Tostig, is virtually the ventriloquist of my cousin, King Edward the Confessor--and now Harold is here, trapped in the lair of the corrupt Count Guy."

William turned to the Sergeant and told him that within the hour they were to ride to the Count's manor near the coast. The Sergeant nodded and moved out.

The Governor stood nearby and wondered if it were really true that William's troops would be vacating his castle before they drank all of his ale from his private reserve, ate all of his food from the cold cellars, and then took all the women by force, who were still hiding in the tunnels – and all the while they would be howling like drunken monsters throughout the night and into the next day. Were they actually leaving? Could this be true? If it were true, then the prayer he made earlier while standing on top of the castle wall had been answered after all, and as a matter of gratitude he vowed to himself to build even more churches throughout the province of Mantes.

"Thank you, Lord! Thank you, Lord! Thank you, Lord!" he was muttering over and over to himself when he was approached by William.

"Governor, we have urgent business to tend to. I'm sorry for the early departure, but..." And at this point the Governor tilted his head to one side and assumed the saddest face that one could ever imagine as William continued, "....but we will return and formalize our earlier agreements regarding protection of the border." The Governor broke into a smile, and was beginning to heap the most lavish praise imaginable on his neighbor when William made a request that came as a hard fist driven deep into the soft pork center of the Governor's solar plexus.

"I've become fond of your wolfhounds, and they of me, and I was wondering if they might accompany me on my short journey to the Count's?"

The Governor knew that if this happened that he would never see his wolfhounds again. The thought of this resulted in the Governor's face being drained of all color; he teetered slightly, and placed a hand against the wall for balance. William noted that it was only a short time ago that the Governor was offering his daughters as hostages, but any mention of his wolfhounds being out of his sight, for even one night, brought the Governor to the brink of keeling over.

William took a step back and examined him: Within an instant the man had become an upright cadaver who had propped himself against a wall so that he wouldn't collapse. His eyes had rolled back in his head, and he was breathing in short gasps.

Now William knew how to control the Governor, and how to make sure that he honored their agreement to protect Normandy's border. He curtly informed The Governor that he could keep his daughters, but the wolfhounds were to become his hostages. Without elaborating William turned and walked away. He heard the Governor cry out, "Please, William! Not my pets… please!" But William called to the wolfhounds, who happily followed their new and far more interesting owner down the hallway and out into the castle yard.

The Governor began to wonder if God had answered his prayers after all, for this is one of the worst things that could have happened to him. He felt that perhaps an earlier declaration that he had made about building churches all over the province of Mantes to show his gratitude to the almighty was made prematurely and out of haste, and just might have to be retracted, or at the very least revised. He would wait to see if William returned his pets to him, then he would make a decision as to whether or not to build more churches.

CHAPTER III

William, Harold, and Count Guy

WILLIAM AND HIS KNIGHTS, AFTER a dusty ride, approached the magnificent country manor of Count Guy, who could be seen near the front gate. The Count was accompanied by a squire, who was shooing away some aggressive geese that had marched forward with their wings spread and their necks extended, hissing in a manner that they hoped would be seen as ferocious. The geese then turned their attention to the wolfhounds, who backed away from these bellicose creatures and stood behind the horses. These were castle dogs whose history was to sleep on large pillows next to the fireplace. At the Mantes Chateau' they were not allowed to mingle with the common barnyard folk, so they stood to one side and eyed the belligerent geese curiously, giving them an occasional faint bark every so often just to keep them away.

The Count was a robust, genteel swindler around forty who greeted William with an artificial joviality that he had seemingly rehearsed over and over from the first moment of his birth.

"Surprise Surprise, surprise! You didn't warn me, otherwise I would have prepared a small banquet for all of you. Greetings, cousin...and I trust—"

But William pushed all of that aside. "I'm not your cousin, and I'm here for the prisoner. Where is he?" demanded William.

"Oh, uh...certainly!" And turning to the squire, said "Squire, bring our guest out, so that we may introduce him to William."

The squire went inside the manor, and Count Guy dropped his voice and continued in a solemn manner: "This unfortunate man, like so many other inexperienced mariners who try to sail our treacherous coast, was lucky to be rescued. It's terrible how many accidents have occurred here lately....God knows I've tried to alleviate the matter by putting up a few lights here and there...but they never seem—"

"How do you know that this is Harold of Essex?" interrupted William.

"By his signet ring...but if you talk to him for only a moment, you can see for yourself." After a trying moment, Count Guy decided to come to the point. His voice elevated a few octaves, and he began by saying,

"Now, William, let me say on this rescuing matter that I'm no profiteer of other people's misfortunes, but there still is a question of expenses incurred here.....do you understand what I'm saying?"

"I think so," answered William. "You want to hand him over to me without a penny of compensation to insure that your well-deserved reputation of generosity survives. Is that it?"

Count Guy threw back his head and forced a laugh. "Well, not exactly, William!"

But at that moment Harold exited the manor, and accompanied by the squire came limping toward them, his hands tied behind his back. The Count had recognized that a complete restoration of his health would insure the maximum recompense, and so Harold had been well tended to in the last several days.

"Why are his hands bound behind his back?" asked William, with undisguised irritation.

The Count, in his haste, had overlooked this small detail. "Why? Why indeed, squire, you ninny?" With that he gave the Squire a vigorous slap on the back of the head, who looked at him in complete surprise. "Don't just stand there, Squire, untie his hands!" added the Count, with feigned outrage.

But William slid off his horse, pulled his knife and walked behind Harold, instantly cutting the bonds. Harold turned to him and thanked him while rubbing his wrists. These two men, as Count Guy and William's soldiers noted, were in many ways the mirror image of one another. Both were tall, fit without being heavily muscled, and well proportioned. Both had strong, angular features, blue eyes, and light hair, though Harold's was streaked with a dark auburn and he had reddish brows.

"I've heard many favorable tales about you, Harold, and at long last I make your acquaintance. I am William, Duke of Normandy. Please accept my hospitality and be the guest of Matilda and me at our castle at Falaise."

"I'd be honored, William," said Harold. William signaled the Sergeant for a horse. The Sergeant dismounted, handing Harold the reins. Count Guy began shifting nervously from one foot to another.

"Pardon me for interrupting, William, but there still is a little matter about the incursion of expenses to be attended to...you see, I don't know—"

But William talked over The Count and looked him straight in the eye while taking a bow and arrow from one of his mounted knights and stringing it.

"But 'not knowing', your Corpulency, can be more enviable than knowing."

"What? I'm sorry! I don't understand. How do you mean?" asked the flustered Count.

William suddenly pointed the arrow straight overhead, pulled the bow to its final length, and fired the arrow high into the air. The Count gasped as he looked skyward, and took a step back, shielding his eyes from the brightness of the sky. Several of the knights sur-reptitiously glanced at one another and then, as incon-spicuously as possible, donned their helmets. Harold seemed more amused than uneasy.

William continued in an easy philosophical tone, directing most of what he said to the Count, while glancing from time to time to his men and Harold.

"I mean my horse, for example, doesn't know that there is an arrow in the sky, probably turning this mo-ment, and is already headed back down towards us. My horse is ignorant of the facts. But it's not the kind of ig-norance that I envy. Let me ask you something, Count. Do you think you can change fate?"

The Count was still shielding his eyes and glancing directly overhead. "I do not!"

"Then you believe that the course of the future is pre-determined?"

"I do."

"Predetermined by whom?"

Count Guy, whose uneasiness has increased in leaps and bounds within the last few seconds, stag-gered backwards while peering into the sky and shout-ed, "I've lost track of it. You haven't changed since you were ten years old, William. This is crazy!"

The Count shrieked, turned and bolted for shelter, but slipped on goose droppings and sprawled face down on the grass. The arrow landed just six inches from his nose, causing The Count, out of sheer terror, to let out a sharp ear-piercing squeal. William and Harold mounted their horses, while the knights had a good laugh; and the knights appreciated the incident as one of the many rewarding perks for riding with The Duke of Normandy – who, in their eyes, was already a legend.

"You see, Harold, the Count says that he believes that his fate was preordained, but if he believed that he could not change his fate, then why did he run?"

William looked around at his knights with a smile. "There you have it! The Count said one thing, yet he does another. The Count hasn't changed since he was ten years old. Avoid him!"

All the knights continued their laughs. William nodded to the squire, who was hiding underneath a tree and advised him to tend to his master, who was still on the ground and ruefully examining his soiled gown.

William and Harold turned their horses and rode out. The knights followed suit, and as they rode out the conversation continued between William and Harold:

"So then, Harold, is the fate of man pre-ordained, as some say, or is man the master of his fate? What do you think?"

"I believe that man should take control of his fate, but there are times when that is impossible."

William smiled and replied, "Well Harold, we'll see if we can devise a test for that? It shouldn't be too difficult."

"You won't have to, William. It's already been put to a test, and the results of the test were irrefutable."

"Really? Tell me about the test, Harold!"

"I can tell you in one word, William."

"Let's hear it!"

"Shipwreck!"

William threw back his head and laughed. "I was not the master of my fate, William!" said Harold, with an engaging smile. After a brief good-natured exchange between the two William rode ahead.

Harold watched as William, from time to time, would dismount his horse, squat down in front of the wolfhounds, and talk to them in a manner as though they perfectly understood his every word. Following that he would do the same with his horse, whispering in his ear and patting him gently on the neck. The stallion would nod, snort, shake his head and paw the grass during these talks, as though he were saying, "So true, William! So true!"

For a man like William, who was stalked by relatives and friends trying to kill him throughout his childhood, the trust that he had with animals far exceeded the trust he had with people. After all, his wolfhounds and his horses would never betray him in a thousand lifetimes, so the emotional life he invested in them would never result in pain and grief.

CHAPTER IV

Harold Meets Adelize and Matilda

WILLIAM AND HIS TWENTY KNIGHTS entered the town of Falaise in late afternoon. The Chateau de Falaise, or simply 'William's Castle', sat on top of a small mountain just south of the center of town. Harold saw immediately that art and beauty were not a priority in William's life. His castle was among the most austere structures that he had ever laid eyes on. Yes, all castles ultimately were bastions, but in the land of the Angles there were prisons that had more interesting lines than this castle. It was as though Odin had showed up carrying a colossal block of limestone, and said, "Here, this will do," and placed a large rectangular block on a mountain top and walked away.

Harold thought that there was no greater key to William's core personality than the design of this castle. Yes, William was a military man for sure, and so a fortress was entirely consistent with his personality. But then Harold began to chastise himself for having these thoughts. He was, after all, deeply honored to be William's guest. If Harold hadn't been born into a family that placed a high value on architectural design he probably wouldn't have noticed these things. He set about to clear his mind of all negative thoughts. It was cluttered with nonsense, he felt, so he wiped it away with the wave of his hand and thought only of the generosity of his new friend, and how fortunate he was to survive the shipwreck, and then be rescued by William from a Count who was holding him for ransom. He had many blessings to consider.

At that moment he caught sight of what had to have been Matilda. She waved to William from the tower with a wide smile, and then ran like a child into the great hallway and out onto the castle bailey, where she continued to wave at her returning hero. This young lady was a beauty. After a moment she was joined by another extremely attractive lady, who stood smiling with her arms folded. This one appeared to be slightly older, perhaps an older sister, he thought; but Harold was soon to learn that he had it all wrong.

The beautiful and lively girl was Adelize, the daughter of William and Matilda. She was a highly precocious young lady; and then there was her mother, Matilda, the one that stood with her arms folded and barely smiling. It was written on her face for all to see that Matilda was married to William, but then William was married to war.

As William and Harold dismounted in the court-yard Matilda said to Adelize, "That must be Harold of Essex." Adelize nodded. Matilda continued, "He's an attractive man, don't you think, Adelize?"

"He's better than most, not as good as some." The truth was that Adelize, on sight was severely struck by Harold, and would remain so for the rest of her life. Matilda turned and re-entered the castle, leaving the infatuated Adelize alone on the balcony. Her father waved to her, and Adelize smiled and waved back.

Harold said, "That must be Matilda."

William chuckled, "No, that's my daughter, Adelize."

"Your daughter? It doesn't seem possible!"

"Matilda and I were married when we were barely older than her. Adelize is seventeen." After a moment, William smiled and asked, "You thought that they were sisters?"

"I did!" answered Harold. "Forgive me!"

William laughed. "Matilda never tires of hearing that, Harold, and neither do I."

That night, with several torches providing the light in the huge hallway, William, Matilda, Harold, and Adelize sat at the warmest end of a lengthy dinner table. The interior of the castle, as Harold reluctantly noticed, was just as austere as the exterior. Harold con-cluded that since William was so often absent, perhaps

Matilda had lost her will to create the palace of her dreams, and simply languished in some kind of fog, lost and disoriented. Later he had learned that in the past she had made modifications to the palace, but he had failed to notice every one of them, and had instead always excused himself to talk to the blacksmiths about new rivets for armor, and other matters that had to do with war.

Here was a young and beautiful princess living in a castle that was owned by a handsome prince that ruled all the land, and all of its people in every direction as far as the eye could see; it was a fairy tale come true... or was it?

Matilda used to see herself, like everyone else in Flanders, as a beautiful girl. That was once upon a time; but now she no longer saw herself that way; and because of William, no man dared look in her direction. She lived in a sort of vacuum. Even on this night, whenever she looked up at Harold, he quickly looked down at his plate to avoid any eye contact. He wanted to make sure that William did not misinterpret a look, a glance, or a tone in his voice.

"Harold, do the Anglish know anything about the false lights that are being put up on the coast so that ships, like yours, will smash on the rocks?" asked Adelize.

William, without looking up, said "It's that fat, sleazy, corrupt Count Guy, who keeps putting up false lights. I should have brought his head back on a pike and made a lantern out of it. Next time I will!"

Harold smiled. "We know about the false lights ruse, Adelize," replied Harold, "but sometimes it's impossible to tell, particularly if the fog is as heavy as it was then. And by the way, I need to notify my people as to the loss. They will be searching for us."

"We have carrier pigeons," said Adelize.

"They'll travel straight to Winchester," added William. "Is that close enough?"

"None better. It's the place of my family," said Harold.

"What family do you have over there, Harold? Are you married? Do you have children?" asked Adelize.

"At the time of his disaster he was probably, like most men, fleeing an entanglement," interjected William.

"Why don't you let him answer for himself, father?" asked Adelize, and turning to Harold, asked "Were you fleeing an entanglement, Harold?"

"I think I was only restless," answered Harold.

"Do you have children?" asked Adelize.

"No."

"Stop badgering the man," demanded Matilda. "Harold, is it Angle Land, or Land of the Angles?" she asked.

"Congratulations, mother, for asking a perfectly boring question? Now he's going to think that we're all a family of lackluster trolls."

"Show some respect, young lady, or I'll send you to your room!"

"Ha! Why don't you put a cap on your head -- with a bell on it -- and do some back handsprings across the floor? What a jester you are tonight!" Adelize said to her mother, while laughing.

"QUIET!" Shouted William, banging his cup on the table, "Or I'll send the both of you to your rooms – and without ale, by god!"

After a tense moment William looked at Harold with a smile and said, "William, when I want to relax, I leave this place and go to war. Death, mayhem, limbs flying past, decapitations, blood spewing everywhere; it's all so relaxing compared to having dinner at my home. I hope you understand now, because these two never will."

"My father thinks he's so amusing," said Adelize, and turning to Harold asked, "I'm wondering why you don't have any children. Is it because you don't want any?"

"Enough, Adelize!" demanded Matilda.

"Well, look at him, Mother. A man as handsome as he is -- and no children? One cannot help but wonder."

"I have to say something now, Harold," interrupted Matilda. "This is what happens when a girl is raised without a father. You can see for yourself that she is without self-control."

"Blame it on me, Matilda! Go ahead! It's all my fault!" shouted William.

"You see what I have to live with, Harold," said Adelize. "All day, every day, they sit around yelling at each other about whose fault it is that I have turned out like this."

Harold found this unforseen exchange somewhat humorous and was dangerously close to spewing ale through his nose. He knew firsthand that it was not unusual for royalty to have these exchanges in private behind closed doors – but this level of volatility around a new guest was unexpected.

William stood up and firmly announced that he was going to take Harold out of the great hall and down into the cellar to see the dragon boat, where a man was safe.

Adelize turned to Harold and said, "That's my father's favorite, taking his friends to see the dragon boat."

"It's the original boat that brought his ancestors here a hundred and fifty years ago," said Matilda.

"I'd consider it an honor," said Harold.

But just then the Sergeant walked in and handed William a message. William promptly handed it to Matilda, who opened it and read, "It's from your old friend, Konan," she said,

"Konan says, 'Greetings Cousin, and I hope all is well. Once again the time has come to reassess our position regarding The Fearless Tower. You are invited to settle this dispute like a man. I know that you'll be here tomorrow by noon, William; because I know that you would rather die in honor than live in shame. Yours truly, Konan."

William turned to Harold, and in an exasperated tone said, "I have cousins everywhere, it seems. My great grandfather, Richard the Fearless of Norway, is also Konan's great grandfather. The dispute with Konan has always been over a structure known as The Fearless Tower, named after our grandfather. It's not far from here, and has always been settled by tournaments."

"That's to prevent a full scale war," added Adelize.

"We'll ride out tomorrow," said William.

And turning to the Sergeant said, "You heard that, Sergeant. I'll need forty knights to ride out by sunrise."

"Is it war, sir?" asked the Sergeant.

"Probably not, but with Konan you can never be sure -- and fetch me the blacksmith, Sergeant!" The Sergeant turned and left. William stood. "You're invited, Harold. You must excuse me now. I have to make preparations."

William turned to Matilda, "And Matilda, please show Harold to his quarters, and why not fix him a horn of ale in the old Norse tradition?"

William nodded to them and walked down the long hallway with his wolfhounds trotting at his side. Adelize stood and yelled after him, "Father, may I show Harold the dragon boat?"

"Excellent idea, Adelize", said William, without turning back. Matilda turned to Harold and said, "You see, Harold. He lurches from one war to the next."

Adelize, leading the way with a torch, descended into a cellar. Harold followed closely behind as they carefully picked their way down a stone stairway with a damp, mossy wall on the left side, and a heavy rusty chain on the right. The heavy moisture in the air made breathing a challenge.

"It used to be dry down here, but with the torrential rains...Ah, here it is. I haven't been down here for a while."

The torch revealed the hull of a boat that when intact was probably fifty feet long. Adelize pointed to the carving on the prow.

"Here's the dragon carving that my father loves so much. It was their symbol." Adelize swung the torch around to a great stone wall where there were many deep carvings of the names belonging to the family tree. The firelight also revealed the many Viking shields with the ancient runic symbols painted on them.

"This is what my father calls the 'Heritage Room'. My father's grandfather's grandfather was a Norwegian Viking by the name of Rolf the Granger. He founded the North Man colony known as Normandy. And there's the name of Richard the Fearless."

Adelize turned to find Harold standing right next to her. While looking into one another's eyes Adelize continued softly,"…and Rolf's grand-daughter was Emma, who is the mother of—"

Harold continued where Adelize left off, "…and Emma is the mother of Edward the Confessor. So Queen Emma of Angle Land is the aunt of William, Duke of Normandy?"

"I thought that you knew that…that my father is the only blood heir to your king, Edward. You didn't know that?"

Harold smiled. "Does your father often talk about his blood ties to the Anglish throne?"

"Yes, he does. Can I ask you something, Harold?"

The torch began to flicker, indicating that a door opened. After a moment Matilda called from above, "Adelize?"

"We'll be up in a minute, Mother." She turned back to Harold. "I just wanted to know…." Adelize broke into an involuntary smile and tried it again, "I just wanted to know…because a friend of my father said that you were known to be seen with a lady by the name of Edith-of-the-Swan's-neck. Is that true?"

"It's true."

"Oh, well…how did she come by that name, if I may ask?"

"She has a neck like a swan."

Adelize tried to smother a laugh, but failed. "I'm sorry. I don't mean to be rude. It doesn't bother her to be called, 'Edith-of-the-Swan's-neck?"

"She has nothing to say about it."

"Oh. I take it that you are not involved with her, then."

Harold smiled. Adelize felt encouraged to continue, "Well, my father doesn't like many people…he speaks highly of you…so we're hoping that you…discover for yourself how hospitable the Normans can be." Her smile widened. Harold noted that Adelize was gazing straight into his soul and not backing down. Matilda once again called for Adelize.

———◆———

That night Harold had fully retired to a luxurious bed. There came a knock on the door. Matilda and Adelize announced to Harold that they had brought his ale. After a moment they quietly entered with Adelize carrying the 'horn of ale' that William had requested for his guest.

"I'm sorry it took so long," said Adelize. "Now tell me if you have anything like this in your Angle Land."

Harold sat up and taking the horn of ale, smelled the aroma of spices native to Normandy. After taking a sip he thought for a moment, while both Adelize and Matilda stood quietly.

"Hmmm....hemlock and nutmeg! Perfect!"

Adelize immediately wheeled on Matilda and pointed accusingly at Matilda, saying "See Mother, you were wrong! He does have a sense of humor after all!"

Matilda's face reddened. "What? I didn't say anything like that!" Flustered, she turned to Harold and began feverishly improvising while giggling, "She's trying to embarrass me. I didn't say anything like that at all." She turned to her daughter and pointed at her, "Whatever you're up to, young lady, it won't work. Off to bed, Adelize!"

But Adelize brushed past this and curtly announced, "I'm going to The Fearless Tower tomorrow."

"Do you have your father's permission?" asked Matilda. "I'm sure that you don't."

"I'll get it tomorrow morning. I don't want to miss out on Konan's vain and boastful swaggering. I wouldn't miss it for anything."

While Adelize was looking in the direction of her mother, this information was solely intended for Harold. Matilda turned to Harold, as Adelize hoped she would, and elaborated: "Konan has been infatuated with Adelize for a long time, but she doesn't seem to be interested in him. It would certainly solve a lot of geographical problems if she were. Brittany would no longer be a thorn in our side."

"Those Kelts down there are all crazy. Besides, he's not for me!" said Adelize, smiling towards Harold with her arms folded.

"Now off to bed, darling," said Matilda.

Adelize nodded in Harold's direction before turning and leaving. After listening to Adelize run up the winding stairs, Matilda turned to Harold and smiled, "She seems intrigued by you."

"Well, if that's the case, then I'm flattered," answered Harold.

Matilda had not failed to notice that Harold had rolled himself up in blankets, rather than climb under them. Matilda recognized this as the habit of the military man who had spent a great deal of his life sleeping on the ground in the rain and snow. She was married to such a man.

"Harold, tell me the truth, now. Are you going to end up sleeping on the floor, because the bed's too soft?"

Harold laughed. "Why do you ask?"

"Because you seem to have a great deal in common with a man that I know," she said, and after a quiet moment Matilda, began again. "Why must you return to Angle Land so soon? What will happen if you don't? Will there be a catastrophe of some kind?

"There's always a catastrophe in Angle Land – several per day. No, the reason is that – I'm missing."

"We've sent the carriers. It only takes them a couple of hours or so to fly the channel – especially in this nice weather. I'm sure that everybody is informed by now, since the messages had the stamp of your signet ring on them."

Harold could easily see that this was a lady who had everything, yet she had nothing. Matilda's life seemed to him to be like a beautiful desert flower that bloomed in the morning sun, and by afternoon she was no longer appreciated by those around her and was tragically wasting away.

"I must return in a couple of days."

"We've had guests stay for months," said Matilda, while taking a seat on the side of the bed.

Harold laughed, "I'm overwhelmed by your kindness and generosity, but I won't be one of those guests."

Jealous beyond description, William was watching Matilda and Harold from a hidden chamber in the castle. It was entirely William's secret. This chamber had been built by Italian artisans while Matilda and Adelize were visiting in Flanders, and the Italian artisans had since returned to their homeland. It was so well hidden that not even his dogs could find it.

As William listened to Matilda, he scrutinized with grief-stricken eyes her every blink and twitch, and carefully monitored the musical swings in her voice. He watched as Matilda put her hand on Harold's and told him that he was welcome to stay as long as he liked, and that there would always be a place for him at the Chateau d' Falaise'.

William's eyes burned with an excruciating pain. He was on the brink of going through the stone wall when Harold began speaking, saying these words:

"Thank you, Matilda. I'm honored. I envy William. He has a wonderful family, a beautiful castle, and he has a reputation as a peerless knight with unparalleled courage and integrity, and I am both honored and proud to be his guest. You are very fortunate to have each other."

Harold withdrew his hand from Matilda's in the pretext of using it to take a sip from the horn of ale.

After hearing these words the searing pain and grief was magically lifted from the eyes of William. He turned away and leaned against the wall of the dark chamber, trying to analyze exactly what this unique physical experience was that he was having. All stress and anxiety had simply melted away. He sat down on the cold dark stone and thought about this: For the first time in his life, a life that knew nothing but treachery and betrayal at every turn since he could remember, he had met someone that he could completely trust – a person that did not have a dagger hidden in their boot. Rare! It had never happened before.

William sat there for a long time turning these things over and over in his mind. He finally concluded that he could not fault Matilda. In some ways he had let her down, and from this day forward he vowed to change his ways. Of course he understood that this would not be an easy challenge, and that this would require a lot of dedication, discipline, and hard work; which reminded him that he had to see the blacksmith about tomorrow's excursion to Konan's.

CHAPTER V

The Green Knight

THE FOLLOWING MORNING FORTY KNIGHTS thundered across the drawbridge. William and Harold rode in front, next to the standard bearer, while Mortaine, a man of the cloth, rode next to the Sergeant. Both he and the Sergeant were riding post. The emblazon bore the Lions of Normandy, with the right paw raised.

From the castle balcony a moist-eyed Adelize watched them ride out; by her dress it looked as though she fully expected to go. Matilda stood next to her and watched the knights as they turned and rode through the south of Falaise, riding four abreast in a column of ten. Matilda took notice as Adelize wiped tears from her cheeks.

"I'm not sure that I understand. Didn't he say that you could go?"

"He said that I could go in a couple of hours. He said that I would be slowing him down, so I am to ride with a couple of the old guards. By the time I get there it'll all be over."

"What will be over?"

"Everything!" Adelize turned and walked back inside the castle.

———◆———

Hawks circled the pale blue western horizon. William and his knights, moving at a slow lope, watched as a large flight of merganser ducks skied into the mirror surface of a small lake. The morning mist was lifting from the water, and shafts of golden sunshine from the east were lighting the verdant countryside.

William glanced at the position of the early morning sun, and using this small, though familiar pond as a reference, calculated the distance made and was happy with it. He was not happy, however, with the healing of his right arm. It had swollen to twice the size of his left, and was throbbing with a pain so intense that he gnashed his teeth as he rode.

But just ahead a knight was sighted, sitting by the side of the road with his face buried in his hands. The knight was dressed from head to toe in green, with a green shield and a green lance that leaned against a nearby ash tree. William gave his knights the signal to halt. The Green Knight looked up at William and his men with blood red grief-stricken eyes that suggested a family tragedy of some kind. William asked the knight if all was well, and if not, could they in any way offer aid. The Green Knight stood and thanked William and his men for their concern. After a moment he introduced himself:

"I am the Green Knight of King Henry's castle, and I left Paris in search of a knight who has the courage and the valor to joust with me. Not easy to find. You see, wherever I go my reputation precedes me."

William had seen hubris a time or two in his life, but this had to be the mother of them all. He began to wonder if this might be the prelude to an ambush, or perhaps something even worse, so he looked carefully around before replying to the Green Knight.

"It's all very clear to me now," began William. "You, my good man, are no longer in the province of Henry's Paris, where a well-known nest of perfumed, dandified fops are known to flourish, and have become as thick as mosquitoes in a late-night swamp. You are now in Normandy, land of the north man, and you are assured of challenges here."

William turned to his knights and said, "Right, men?" All the knights cheered and banged their lances against their shields.

The Green Knight smiled, and in an instant the dark clouds in his life began to lift. William continued: "But why squander your sorrow here at the side of the road, Green Knight? You are welcome to join us, as we are on our way to engage Konan, at the River of the Fearless Tower."

In a flash the Green Knight's eyes were transformed from sorrow to jubilation. He could barely contain himself, and stuttered as he asked, "Terra major, or border skirmish, good sir?"

"Border skirmish!"

"Konan, you say? Could it be Konan the Kelt?"

"The same, but he's changed his name to Konan the Great."

The Green Knight smiled brightly and said that he was deeply honored by the invitation, and told the knights that he would strike his pavilion and catch up with them. William's knights saluted the Green Knight and rode away while the elated Green Knight, with great haste, set about to strike his pavilion before scrambling for his war horse.

His war horse had been standing nearby and, while chewing slowly, was pretending to be bored, but was actually weighing all that was said with a keen interest.

CHAPTER VI

Matilda and Spanish Dancer

ADELIZE IMPATIENTLY TAPPED HER FOOT in the castle courtyard. She was fashionably dressed for the ride, with a parasol, a bonnet, and a special riding dress of some kind. Several fit guards stood nearby, waiting to escort her to the River of the Fearless Tower. Her mother walked up behind her and asked Adelize what she was doing.

"My father said that as soon as the shadow from this stick hits this rock, then I can go.

"How insane!"

"You're so right, Mother." Adelize bent down and slid the rock into the shadow of the stick. "There! It's time to leave."

With the help of a squire Adelize began mounting her horse. Matilda said, "Wait one minute and I'll go with you." She had turned and was walking away when Adelize said, "I don't want you to take this wrong, Mother, but I'll be riding fast, and I don't want to be standing by all the time while you're trying to catch up."

After a moment Matilda quietly said to her, "That might be the most insulting thing that you have ever said to me. We'll see who waits for who?" And turning to the squire said, "Squire, fetch me Spanish Dancer." The squire hesitated, and then looked toward Adelize for help, but Matilda was resolute and smashed her riding crop against the side of a fence rail. "Do it now, squire!"

The squire moved out toward the livery stable. Adelize leaned forward and said, "Mother, don't be ridiculous!"

"Don't wait for me! Go on! I'll catch up with you." Matilda turned and briskly walked across the courtyard and into the castle with Adelize yelling after her,

"Even father has a hard time with Spanish Dancer!" yelled Adelize. But Matilda continued on without a glance in her direction. Adelize turned her horse and galloped toward the livery where she caught up with Squire Dudley, who anticipated Adelize's request and held up his hand to calm her.

"You know your mother was a jumping champion in Flanders, don't you? That's how your parents met."

"I know all that, but—"

The squire walked a tightrope, being firm, while maintaining respect at the same time.

"She gave it up because of you, Adelize. She was carrying you at the time, and she didn't want to lose you. I know, because I was there. You're forgetting that I was a friend of her father's."

"I'm not forgetting that, squire, and I appreciate your concern, but you know that Konan gave that horse to my father to get even with him, don't you?"

"Yes, I know that, Adelize. I was there when it happened. But don't worry, my lady. She's not going to be climbing on the back of the Andalusian. I'll make sure of that.....and if I don't –, "The squire nodded in the direction of the stables and continued, "--he will!"

Spanish Dancer

Adelize turned to see the huge black Andalusian stallion with a single white sock trotting in a circle behind a high fence with its ears laid back. It snorted, tossed its head, and then suddenly spun in two rapid circles. Adelize shook her head, "That horse is mentally ill."

"Whoa! Not so loud!" warned the squire. "He's acting that way because he knows we're talking about him."

"Nonsense! That crazy horse doesn't know how to do anything but eat and sleep." At that moment Spanish Dancer went berserk, kicking walls, raring on its hind legs, knocking down posts, and then gloriously prancing sideways while tossing his head and snorting. The squire concealed his smile by turning his head away from Adelize.

The princess commented further. "We have to return that thing to Konan." said Adelize, who adjusted her skirt and parasol before turning her delicate palfrey in the direction of the western horizon. She nodded to the squire and began her journey, trotting sidesaddle in the direction of Konan's tournament, and flanked by four knights instead of the usual two.

———————◆———————

Gathered near the Fearless Tower were William, Harold, The Green Knight, and William's forty knights. On the western side of the tower were Konan and the Keltic lancers of approximately the same number. The Kelts had their insignias tattooed on their bodies in the form of Keltic spirals and triskelions, and some had these insignias painted on their warhorses as well. Many of the Kelts had their hair spiked with lime so that it stood straight up. Konan himself was a well-muscled and natural born agitator. He, like William, was already a living legend among his people. Konan opened the dialogue with a jibe,

"I see that you didn't appreciate my gift."

"The horse?"

"Yes. Spanish Dancer! Where is he?"

"I reserve him for professional guests, the ones who I never want to see again."

Konan and his men laughed at this.

"My messengers tell me that we have two new guests today – The Green Knight, and Harold of Winchester."

"Aye!" said William. "They are my friends."

Konan nodded to them both, and then spoke to The Green Knight in the native tongue of the Kelts, asking him if he were a Highlander. The Green Knight replied in the Gaelic of the Highlanders. Both the Green Knight and Konan nodded respectfully toward one another. Konan turned to Harold, saying these words:

"Well, if it's agreeable to you, Cousin William, we'll determine who the Fearless Tower belongs to for the coming year by a jousting tournament--let the gods decide!"

"I know who it belongs to, Konan--that's not a matter for the gods to decide. I'm here because when my knights are idle, they tend to maim and kill one another; so to save my knights from extinction, I have to take them on a wild pig hunt from time to time."

Konan laughed uncomfortably. William turned to his knights, asking "Well, how about it, knights? Feel like jousting?"

The knights shouted their approval while banging their lances against their shields. William turned back, "It's decided by acclamation, Konan. Jousting it is!"

"Then it's to the jousting field!" And turning to his men, Konan yelled, "Ho, Lancers!" The Keltic lancers let out the Keltic war cry and put their horses into a wild gallop, heading for the jousting field. William and his forty knights were close behind.

———◆———

Adelize, sitting primly on her palfrey and seemingly conscious of fashion, was flanked by two knights on each side. The knights were intent on pampering Adelize throughout her journey, inquiring as to her needs, her comfort, whether or not she was thirsty, or if she would like to stop and rest, or if she desired an extra cushion under her seat, or if she wanted someone to hold the parasol over her head so that she could rest her weary limbs, and so on and so forth, when behind them they heard something that sounded like a roll of thunder. All turned to look. The rolling thunder was nothing more than horses hooves – Spanish Dancer's -- who in his surge for freedom, was like an eagle newly released from captivity, whose heart soared with an exhilaration that Homer on his best day could not describe.

"Oh no!" whispered Adelize.

"Do you recognize the rider?" asked a knight, while pulling his sword.

"Holy Mother of God, it's my mother, and she's on Spanish Dancer!"

All the knights were frozen as ice sculptures as they watched the rider descend a faraway hill, churning up dust and moving toward them like a raging ball of fire.

Though Matilda knew horses well, and had been a champion in her day, this one was unlike anything that she had ever ridden. She had early on in this journey abandoned the idea of controlling Spanish Dancer. His massive neck was twice the size of the Flemish jumping horses that she had once known, and he could not be controlled by her. She was simply a passenger along for the ride. Once she realized that Spanish Dancer opted to stay in the middle of the road and not run wildly through the brush and trees she began to relax and wait for him to tire; the only problem with this line of thought was that the huge Andalusian seemed tireless.

This particular Andalusian was a known giant among his own breed, tall and muscular, but mentally deranged from inbreeding, so said the experts. Yet Matilda had never ridden a horse that ran so fast, so furious, and whose gait was air smooth – a genuine Pegasus! She felt as though she were having the greatest dream of her life, and experiencing all the beauty of an unexplored life that lay beyond the castle walls in a way that could never have been concocted or imagined -- even by all of the sorcerers of Normandy.

It soon came to Matilda, that they were both, after all, freedom seekers; and that she was riding on the back of a fellow refugee. She felt that he had, in some way, recognized this, otherwise he could have easily thrown her off long ago. As she approached Adelize and the four knights it occurred to Matilda that she didn't want to appear as an unwilling passenger on a runaway horse, so when she got close enough for them to hear, she began to yell, while flashing her riding crop from side to side,

"Show me who you are, stallion of Spain, and I promise I will do the same for you."

"HIIIIYYYYYAAAA! HIIIYYYYAAAA! FASTER DANCER! FASTER!" she yelled, and then quietly in his ear she whispered, "Show me who you are, stallion of Spain, and I promise I will do the same for you!"

He must have heard her, for there was a surge of strength and speed that astonished Matilda. To her amazement Spanish Dancer had only been cruising, and it was fortunate for the Duchess that she'd had a firm grip on his mane with both hands, otherwise she could have been left behind.

The two flew past Adelize and the four knights in a whirl of dust, which ripped the parasol from Adelize's hands and spun it into a nearby field. They watched as Matilda lay flat and low on the back of the over-sized Spanish bred warhorse; and with hooves thundering down the long road, Adelize and her knights stood numb as the two runaways disappeared over a distant hill.

Sometime later, in the middle of a cold water stream, Matilda slid off the mountain of a horse and dropped trembling to her hands and knees, where she drank alongside the Andalusian. After a while she plunged her head into the cold water, allowing the icy current to swirl around her nose and eyes for some time before rising to her feet and wringing her hair while taking a look around.

Then an odd thing happened: She started crying and could not stop. This was something that she could normally will away, but for some reason this time it wasn't working. She dropped the reins to the horse and stepped to the shore. She felt silly. This crying had to come to an end, especially since there was no reason for it. After a moment she wiped away tears, and she had begun wringing the final droplets out of her hair when she felt a nudge on her back. It was him, Spanish Dancer. Was he asking her if everything was alright? She stroked his nose and talked to him as an old friend while scanning the area for a small tree to climb. There it was, with a perfectly shaped overhead branch. That was the one that she would climb, like she did as a child in Flanders, and then the child would lower herself onto the back of the giant Andalusian so that they could continue their journey. It had been a long time since she had mounted a horse in this manner. Matilda, on this day, realized that she had rediscovered the child in herself. It was a good day.

CHAPTER VII

Konan the Great and the

Fearless Tower

KONAN THE KELT, NOW KNOWN by some as "Konan the Great", spared no expense when it came to the training of his knights. His jousting field, he mandated, was to serve as an example of excellence among all fighting men to the rest of the Gaelic lands, and especially neighboring Paris, which he felt was growing soft and sliding into mediocrity. The greatest Kelt of them all,

The Welsh Dragon of Arthur

KING ARTHUR OF WALES, WHO had lived five hundred years earlier, was of exactly the same blood.

The Kelts of Brittany had fled Caesar a thousand years earlier, and had crossed the channel to southwest England, where there were already flourishing Keltic populations, as described by Caesar in his great book, *The Gallic Conquest*. After that the island, which had been called by some, "Albion", was eponymously named "Britain", according to the druid scholars of the province of Brittany.

The Welsh King Arthur

Konan continually reminded his men that they had much to live up to; but this they already knew, for just as the Greeks knew Homer, and the Romans knew Virgil, the Kelts were all very well versed regarding the campfire tales of King Arthur, Vercingetorix, Boudicca, Lancelot, Korreus the Kelt, and many others. From time to time Konan and a select few would take a pilgrimage with the Druids of Brittany to the island across the channel and visit Stonehenge, an ancient celebratory gathering place for those of the Keltic lands.

———◆———

The stands of the jousting field were replete with knights, damsels, and squires on Konan's side. On William's side were the same, minus the damsels. Konan gave his inspirational talk to several of his lancers from his position on the stands.

"Our greatest danger is in overconfidence, lancers. Do not underestimate these Normans; essentially they are Vikings on horseback. They have great intelligence, they train hard, and they have the will to win. Summon all resources, and may the gods be with us."

During this a druid whose face could not be seen beneath his dark hood sprinkled magic water on each knight while softly muttering words in the ancient tongue.

William was also concerned about over-confidence. His men had never known defeat. They were beginning to feel that defeat was something that could never happen to them -- no matter what. They had seen days where everything went wrong, and they, the invincible men of the north, had still crushed their opponents, putting out the fires of their enemy's history forever. William's concern was that this put his men in danger of getting lazy and losing focus.

"These Kelts are the sons of Arthur. They are the Excalibur of mankind. They are highly skilled and infinitely courageous. Do not underestimate them! Fight on for Normandy, and may Odin be with you, blessed knights."

Normandy, like many European provinces, was still in a period of transition between the Norse gods and Christianity, so they would appeal to one or the other depending on the circumstance. On this day there was much talk of Odin and Thor among the Norman knights, even though Mortaine, a disciple of LanFranc's, was traveling with William to offer his Christian blessings.

All the knights of the field banged their lances together and turned their destriers in the direction of the start area. The others took a seat in the stands, which sat opposite the Kelts.

William turned to the Green Knight and said, "And I'm sure that you will understand, sir, when I tell you that the first challengers will be my hand-picked Normans." The Green Knight unhappily nod-ded his understanding and took a seat in the stands directly behind William. William was seated next to Harold, Mortaine, the Sergeant, and the rest of the knights.

The ram's horn was blown as a signal for the knights to line up in opposition. The announcement was made that the contest would feature a single Keltic lancer against a single Norman knight. The ram's horn was blown again and the knights charged one another. The Keltic lancer unhorsed the Norman knight.

The field was cleared and the ram's horn was blown once again, and once again the knights charged one another on their warhorses. Another Keltic lancer unhorsed another Norman knight, and then another, and yet another. William and his knights were solemn, while Konan and his entourage of damsels, lancers, and druids waved their flags and danced with joy on the opposing benches.

In the midst of their celebration a Keltic Lancer sighted an approaching rider. The rider was Matilda. She had not been able to stop the horse, so she opted to ride straight though the jousting field and out the other side, flashing her riding crop from side to side and yelling, "HIYYYYYYAAAAAAAAA!", as though she were simply out for a casual ride.

Because Matilda weighed half as much as any of the men that were in full fighting gear, she passed through at a speed that had seldom been seen by either knights or lancers.

Konan yelled to William, "What was that?"

William smiled, and cupping his hands called back, "I think it was, my wife, Matilda, out for her afternoon ride on the horse you gave us -- Spanish Dancer."

"Spanish Dancer?"

"Yes. He proved too tame for me and my knights--- we gave it to the women...as a starter. But thank you for the gift anyway, Konan. I know you meant well."

Harold turned his head away from the bewildered Konan and smothered an involuntary laugh. William, with a sense of urgency, spoke in confidence to a couple of his mounted knights, one of whose name was Tremaine.

"Catch up with her, Tremaine, and bring her back!" The knights rode out and the tournament was resumed.

William watched as the Keltic Lancer across the field trotted over to Konan and conferred with him. This lancer who had defeated one Norman knight after another was known as Koreus the Kelt.

All brave Kelts knew the story of Koreus: Koreus was named after a famous Keltic hero that fought, singlehandedly, Caesar's men to a draw. They offered him free passage if he would only surrender. Koreus declined. Finally, because none of Caesar's soldiers could defeat Koreus in a fair fight, the black-hearted Caesar had him taken down at a distance that was safe for his men -- with arrows. Koreus, after that, was not referred to by name by any of Caesar's soldiers, but only as "The man that could not be bought", which to some, reflected the highest quality in a man, and was the greatest of all honors.

Koreus and the Norman Knight charged one another. The Norman was again unhorsed by Koreus. William was completely vexed, and turned to Harold for a possible insight:

"Harold, never before have Norman knights fallen like ninepins. Normandy has never been so disgraced. What could be the problem?"

Harold was evidently uneasy with the task of offering an explanation and hesitated before answering. "It seems to me, sir, that perhaps your knights are too upright—, "but Harold was interrupted with a derisive laugh from the Green Knight.

"Pardon me, William, but the observations of a... choir boy at a time like this hardly seem appropriate. Mind if I make an observation, William?"

"Proceed, Green Knight!"

"I'm seeing something. The Kelts are carrying their lances high, luring your knights into defending their head, then a split-moment before impact they drop point to the groin and lunge forward to extend their length slightly. I can take them, sir. May I try?"

William didn't like relegating his honor to one of King Henry's Parisian knights, but at the moment what else could he do? He nodded in affirmation.

The Green Knight swung out from a nearby post and landed on his charger like a man who had only a single interest in life. A knight pitched him his green helmet from his pavilion, while another Norman handed the Green Knight his lance and shield.

His war horse arched his neck and began to prance as the Green Knight spoke gently to him and told him to be patient. "Soon enough! Soon enough!" he kept repeating over and over to his eager destrier. The Green Knight turned and flashed a winning smile to the Normans. He was a man in his late twenties, with dark hair, green eyes, a strong chin, and like all knights now and forever, had a slender build.

Konan taunted William, "Ha! Do the Normans really have to reach into King Henry's pockets, William? Where are those Norman heroes I have been hearing so much about?"

The Green Knight and Konan had a brief and highly volatile exchange in Gaelic before the Green Knight turned and took his position at the starting gate.

William angrily stood up. Konan had crossed the line. He would have leapt into the arena himself, had it not been for his severely injured right arm from the castle siege at Mantes.

Koreus the Kelt, who was confidently riding on a string of victories that he'd had against the Norman knights, now raised his visor so that the Green Knight, who was standing downfield and opposite of him, could look into his eyes and see for the last time the man that would finally disgrace him. Koreus wore only chest armor with no protection for his tattooed arms and shoulders. He was confident that there was not a man born who could unhorse him, and the Green Knight had the same confidence in his abilities.

The Green Knight

The ram's horn blew once again, and the warhorses burst from their gates with their necks arched, their nostrils dilated, and a raging fire in their eyes. Both knights, as they approached one another, felt that they had sensed the other's weakness as they charged forward, and then

WHAM!

The Green Knight unhorsed Koreus the Kelt, ending his string of victories against the Normans. The Normans were beside themselves with joy. The Kelts were in shock.

Konan's younger brother, Getorix the Swift, vaulted the rail of the stands with his left arm and landed on the back of his destrier, which like him, was heavily painted with blue triskelions. Getorix fastened his upper body armor with the help of his aides, and then declined his mask. Konan stood and signaled a stop to this, but too late! Getorix, without waiting for the ram's horn charged the Green Knight. The Green Knight turned his destrier and charged. The two met in the center and

WHAM!

The Green Knight flew Getorix the Swift, who landed near the feet of the Keltic stands. The damsels screamed, the lancers shouted their outrage, and things were very close to spinning out of control when Konan did a running leap from the stands and landed on the back of his warhorse. His horse spun twice in the center of the ring, and he threw his armored glove high into the air, which landed at the feet of the Green Knight's horse.

"You are challenged, peacock!"

The Green Knight threw back his head and laughed. He was fully aware that war could easily break out with these hot heads, so he tried to keep things civil. He nodded his head and with an even tone in his voice said to Konan, "I graciously accept your challenge, good sir, and it will be an honor to joust with Konan the Great!"

Konan returned to the starting position. All eyes were on Konan. His upper body was heavily muscled, and his hair was spiked straight up with lime. He wore the blue Keltic spirals on each cheekbone, with the teeth of the Euro-wolf hung around his neck. He fastened the armor for the upper body, but declined all other armor, including the protective mask and helmet. William was about to call a halt to this madness, when, without waiting for the ram's horn, Konan let out a war cry and charged the Green Knight. The Green Knight spun his destrier and charged. Both met in the center, and

WHAM!

Konan flew the Green Knight, who landed in a tangled heap near the stands of the Normans. The outraged Norman knights leaped into the jousting arena with their swords drawn. The Keltic lancers drew their swords and leaped into the arena as well. A slaughter was only seconds away when the lovely Duchess of Normandy known as 'Matilda' rode into the center of the ring on Spanish Dancer, escorted by Tremaine and another guard.

Suddenly all went quiet. Tremaine dismounted and ran to her, ready to be of assistance; but Matilda didn't need it. She slid off of the huge Andalusian and dropped to the ground like a cat. William thought that he noticed an ever so slight exchange of smiles between Matilda and Tremaine as she nodded her thanks. Matilda then turned and smiled at William.

She, for some reason, looked like the day that he first met her. Her long blonde hair was wild and tangled, her blue eyes alive, sparkling and foxy, and she once again wore the playful smile that she had become famous for in her youth. William helped her into the stands, wondering if this new look might be the result of a quiet sexual escapade of some kind, possibly with the unbearable smoothie who called himself 'Tremaine'.

The Green Knight was on his feet, slightly shaken, but still every bit the smiling and confident Green Knight as he bowed to the cheers and applause from both Normans and Kelts.

Matilda sat next to William and took hold of his arm, seeing that he was despondent. William told her that this day would live in infamy, and that they were both dishonored. "I would give my entire kingdom if my damaged arm could hold a lance today." Matilda held him close and said, "Stop it, William!"

A show of civility soon resumed in the arena. Konan, after congratulating the Green Knight on a battle well fought, turned to William and said,

"Well William, the gods have made their decision: The Fearless Tower belongs to the Kelts for the coming year. Your men did well, but not well enough, and I—"

But a gauntlet landed at the feet of Konan.

CHAPTER VIII

The Black Knight

ALL TURNED TO SEE HAROLD as he approached Konan. From the distance of a lance he quietly said, "I would be deeply honored if you would accept my challenge, Konan."

Konan smiled and nodded. "Challenge accepted, Harold, and who do you fight for, Angle Land?"

"On this day I fight for Normandy, and for the honor of my friends, William and Matilda."

"Challenge accepted," said Konan, "and may your Valkyries be with you, because Victoria, the Goddess of Victory, is already mine!"

Konan turned and trotted to the Keltic side.

William stood and stepped in front of Harold, blocking his path. "I'm sorry Harold. I can't let you do this. You've barely recovered from the shipwreck—"

"Sorry William. Any other time I would listen to you, but I can't now." And turning to Matilda asked, "Matilda, with your permission I would like to ride your destrier."

"Permission granted, Harold!" answered Matilda, and turning to William requested that he sit down and watch the final joust of the day.

William reluctantly took a seat as he watched Harold jump into the arena and walk toward Spanish Dancer; but Spanish Dancer didn't know this one and laid his ears back. Matilda saw this and ran down the steps into the arena to Spanish Dancer. She approached him and spoke quietly to him; Harold waited patiently while Matilda worked her magic with Spanish Dancer.

In the meantime Harold had seen another of William's knights dressed in black, and he had requested the use of the knight's black armor. That armor was immediately surrendered by the knight and was being fitted to Harold by William's aids as Harold continued to introduce himself to the warhorse. Harold quietly talked to Spanish Dancer and stroked his nose, while Matilda patted the side of his neck and whispered to him. After a while Matilda nodded to Harold. Spanish Dancer had granted him permission, she said, with a short laugh -- as though in jest, yet she meant every word of it.

Konan wasn't taking any chances. He had a strange feeling about this Harold of Winchester, whose name was familiar to him. But it was hard to read this man: Was this the same carousing, fighting, jousting, hard drinking and wenchifying Harold that would disappear from his land for months at a time, fighting nameless in tournaments anywhere from The Black Forest to

Flanders? Whatever the case, today's event had mostly been decided….mostly. He had to close this one out with a clean victory. All of this nonsense about 'North Man greatness' was wearing the Kelts down, and today that line of thought happily was about to come to an end. Konan's aids sensed this, and were like a hive of enthusiastic bees running a checklist to make sure that all fighting gear was properly fitted and fastened.

But a new arrival turned all heads and in an instant not a single person thought of anything else but Princess Adelize. Looking like a royal princess that had descended from her mountaintop down through the clouds to mingle with the common folk, she nodded, smiled, and waved in all directions; and she waved and nodded to both Konan and Harold before being helped down by a rush of eager knights, who slavishly surrounded her and helped her to dismount her palfrey.

Princess Adelize took a seat next to Matilda and William, and before Adelize could congratulate her mother on still being alive and well, she received the grim update on the Norman defeat in the day's joust. William once again repeated his angst regarding his injury, and confided to them that he would like nothing more than to fly Konan from his horse – something the both of them already knew, but they nodded their heartfelt understanding anyway.

Adelize, after a few moments learned that Harold was about to joust with Konan. This was a revelation that came as a shock to Adelize. William further informed her that they had already lost The Fearless Tower, and that Harold had volunteered in the final joust of the day to recover it. Adelize had serious doubts about this joust and was on the brink of protesting to William, but in the end decided to stay quiet, knowing full well that she would never be able to stop the contest, and if she interfered it could very well throw Harold off of his game and make matters much worse. She opted to stay out of it completely; but for a beautiful young princess like Adelize, things were never that easy.

Konan, now combat ready, began prancing in circles in the center of the jousting area, and finally made his way over to Adelize.

"I bid you good day, Adelize. You're just in time to see the finale – that is, Normandy's final disgrace is about to begin."

Adelize smiled, and returned the jest, "There is a type of mushroom that is common in this part of Brittany that causes one to have wild dreams and visions, I hear. Perhaps you've had a few too many of those mushrooms, Konan."

Konan laughed, along with the others. After a moment of smiling he continued, "I would like to volunteer my services as your champion against the Saxon, Adelize."

Konan saw her hesitate. This had never happened before. Adelize had always allowed Konan to fight as her champion. It was all in good fun to her, but for Konan it had always meant something more, so he continued:

"Fairest Adelize, all dissent between Brittany and Normandy would vanish if you would only allow me to be your champion."

It seemed to Matilda and William that Konan was actually suggesting that he would be willing to forfeit the ownership of The Fearless Tower for another year if Adelize would only give Konan permission to fight for her. They both turned to her…and waited.

Finally Adelize stood and untied her scarf. Konan smiled and lowered his lance so that she could tie the scarf around it. He would then swing it upright, and the scarf would slide down the lance and around his arm, where he would tighten it with his free hand, as they had done so often in the past.

But this day was different. "Thank you, Konan, but I'm spoken for."

With these words she held up her scarf to Harold, who was dressed from head to toe in black, with a black helmet and a black lance. He was sitting perfectly still on top of Spanish Dancer at the starting gate. When Harold saw Adelize waving to him he removed his helmet and trotted over to her family's tournament box. Once there he lowered his lance in a way that suggested that this was not the first time he had been a lady's champion. Adelize loosely tied the scarf around the tip. Harold tipped the lance upward, and the scarf slid down around his arm. While tightening the scarf he told Adelize that he was deeply honored, turned his destrier and then galloped back to the starting position. William and Matilda exchanged clandestine glances.

Konan seethed. The blood of his Keltic ancestors burned like a white-hot fire within him.

Konan turned his horse in a fury and sprinted across the jousting field, knocking down all standing Keltic shields with his lance at a full run. He turned and galloped across the field and knocked all of the Norman shields down with his lance. A cheer went up from the Kelts, and they began pounding their swords against their shields while chanting, "Death to the Black Knight! Death to the Black Knight!"

Konan returned to his starting position. As Konan's attendants swarmed their hero, a sage whispered advice in his ear. "See how this Harold couches his lance? This one will use the old German method, my liege."

Konan nodded his understanding, and in an unusual drift toward the analysis of the technique of others, concurred with the sage, "Aye! It's the Black Forest Method. They lunge forward and the shock of the lance is taken entirely with the stirrups. It's difficult to perfect, but that's how they of the Black Forest fly their opponents."

"Exactly," concurred the sage. "With the old German method, timing is everything."

Konan was lowered onto his charger, and his lance was handed to him by the sage, who gently knocked on Konan's helmet, and then in a hushed and confidential manner he said to him,

"This is the lance of good fortune, Konan. Mark the length well." Konan accepted the lance without looking at it. Konan knew what it was. It had an illegal extension on it, which would alter the timing of the impact by a split-second. He felt ashamed of himself for not returning it to the sage, but in today's contest the tension was unusually high, and there was so much at stake....the Fearless Tower, the dignity of Brittany, the reputation of his lancers, his esteem as a leader equal to that of William's, and most importantly the heart of Adelize.

For the first time in years he felt a surge of undiluted fear rip through his soul. This fear was not to be mistaken for a lack of confidence; it was simply the body's way of telling the mind to summon all resources for this event. Konan the Great, like all fighting men, welcomed the injection by his system that heightened his awareness. It would give him additional strength, courage, and focus. Without it, he would be less of a fighting man.

The ram's horn was blown and the warhorses leaped forward. The crowd noticed that Spanish Dancer was nearly at full speed after three leaps. Both knights bore down on each other, lowering their lances and couching them on the approach.

WHAM!

Both Harold and Konan were hit. Konan flew high before hitting the ground, while Harold swung wide from his saddle but managed to swing back to an upright position, surviving the brutal impact.

The Black Knight unhorses Konan the Great

The Normans jumped to their feet and cheered wildly. The Kelts rushed to Konan, who pushed them away and insisted that he climb to his feet without aid. After brushing his fellow lancers away Konan stood on his own, nodded to the crowd, and both

Normans and Kelts applauded the bravery of Konan. Konan held up both hands and quieted the cheering on both sides.

"The Black Knight has fought with courage and honor. I, Konan the Great of Brittany, now declare Normandy the winner of the tournament – and the Black Knight its champion." Again both Kelts and Normans banged their lances against their shields and cheered wildly. Adelize, William, Matilda, the Green Knight, Mortaine and the Sergeant walked on the field to congratulate their new hero. But as they approached Harold they saw him sway, and then his lance and shield dropped to the ground. Harold slumped over and fell from his horse, hitting the ground at Konan's feet. The Normans rushed to assist Harold.

The Green Knight saw something interesting on the ground. It was the broken shaft of Konan's lance, and there it was, for all to see – the illegal extension. He picked it up and turned it over and over.

Konan saw this, excused himself from his attendants, and walked over to him. The Green Knight saw him approaching and braced himself. This would be a fight to the death, but then an unexpected thing happened. Konan stood in front of the Green Knight, and after a quiet moment said these words:

"I have lived my entire life placing honor above everything else. Honor has been the guiding force for every decision I have ever made in my life. But to-day I failed myself. I think that the love of a woman will sometimes drive a man to do things, both good and bad, that he is otherwise incapable of doing. My heartfelt apologies to Harold, to William, to Adelize, to Matilda, to all Normans, and to you, Green Knight, who has brought honor and courage to my home in the Land of the Kelts."

If the nine Valkyries had swooped down and snatched the Green Knight and had taken him for a ride to Valhalla, he couldn't have been more surprised than when he heard these words spoken by Konan. Disdain morphed into admiration, and after a moment he handed the broken lance to Konan. "This belongs to you, and we will never speak of it again – and now I know why they call you 'Konan the Great'. Just now you exhibited more courage than I have seen in all of the day combined, Konan. I consider you a brother."

The pain in Konan's eyes vanished, and was re-placed by a deep respect for this mysterious knight who traveled the lands of Europe without a name.

"Please know that you will always have a home in Brittany, Green Knight."

The entire conversation between the two had taken place in Gaelic. The two clasped hands and then the Green Knight turned in the direction of Harold, who was being carried toward a pavilion.

He could see that druids were standing by with the bark of a willow tree and other herbs to ease the pain before removing the tip of the lance, which had broken off inside of Harold.

CHAPTER IX

Tostig; the Diving Duck

BEYOND THE ANGLE LAND VILLAGE of Winchester on the River Itchen an ivy covered grey stone manor with steep roofs sat cold and lonely on a dark and windy day. The trees were bent over by the wind, the river had whitecaps, and some of the peasants in town were busy chasing their thatched roofs, which had blown off their structures. There was no lightning and thunder on this day, only a driving rain and an incessant wind that howled without pause; it was a demonic howling that would rise and fall in a way that suggested that the wind itself was grieving over a heavy loss of some kind and out of anger decided to punish all forms standing in its path.

But it was a good day for those who were indoors next to a raging fire, like Tostig, brother of Harold; and Baron Angsley, who was playing chess with Tostig. Perkins of Anglia, who had won not many games in his life, was happy to sit next to both of them and give advice on where to move. He felt that his luck was much better on the sidelines than actually playing.

Sitting not far away by the massive fireplace was Judith of Flanders, Tostig's wife. She used to conceal her boredom with artificial laughs and smiles, but that was during their courtship. Now that she was married she openly advertised her boredom by sighing in front of guests and slamming doors.

Sitting next to a large arched window was Bishop Verser, Harold's good friend since childhood. He was a man of the cloth, but he was also a gifted scribe who penned legal documents for the Godwinson family. Harold felt that there was not a more trustworthy man that could be found on the entire island of Albion than Bishop Verser. Most people would agree to that assessment, including Bishop Verser, whose life's work, for him, was to set the example for the meaning of the word 'honor'.

Tostig held up his hand. "That's not allowable! Put it back, Baron!"

"Why?" asked the Baron.

"Because you've moved the rook! Now you can no longer castle!"

"Tostig is right!" said Perkins. "You've moved the king's rook!"

"Nonsense!" and turning to the Bishop, "Bishop Verser, we need a ruling, sir."

Without looking up Bishop Verser agreed that once the king's rook was moved then The Baron could no longer castle kingside. The Baron turned back to scrutinizing his position on the board, saying "This is bad! This is very bad!" Tostig rubbed his hands together in anticipation of a victory and called to his wife, "Judith dear, would it be possible to have a refill of that wonderful hot spicy drink for our guests – and I'll have a refill too, if you would be so kind?" Judith stood up, and without looking at anybody announced that she was bored. She left the room and slammed the door on the way out. She was not seen or heard from for the rest of the day.

The Baron shook his head and then returned to staring at the board. Tostig, after a moment of silence commented to the others. "Remember how Judith was before I married her? She was a servant, a court jester, a minstrel, a bard, a nurse, and a delightfully crude tart all weaved into a very fine paradigm of womanhood."

"I remember that!" said Perkins.

"And royalty to boot! 'Judith of Flanders', for god's sake!" said the Baron without looking up.

"She needs a challenge," said Perkins. "I know women like no man that you have ever known", he said while flashing his near perfect teeth. "Women need a challenge. The first time that you tell them that they're beautiful, they're wonderful, and that all is well, that's when they start sulking around and slamming doors! I've seen it a thousand times."

"But you've never been married, Perkins."

"Exactly!" said Perkins. "That way I am always seen as a challenge."

"Is this the man that's giving me advice on my chess game?" asked the Baron, while looking around to the others. "It's no wonder that I'm losing!"

"I'll give her a challenge," said Tostig, in his customary nasal whine. "I'll give her a one-way swim across the channel back to Flanders! It's your move, Baron!"

"She'll never fetch the hot spiced drink, Tostig," said Perkins. "I'll get it myself. In fact, I'll get a cup for all of us. How's that for service?"

"You'll poison it, Perkins, to get me out of the way so that you can have Judith all to yourself," said Tostig.

Baron Angsley burst out laughing at this and with a wave of the hand conceded the game to Tostig. Perkins left the room to get the hot spiced drinks while the Baron leaned back in his chair and asked Tostig, "Still haven't heard from your brother, Harold?"

"He's off on one of his tangents, somewhere, probably hallucinating in a cave near the Irish Sea, or something like that."

"Or he could have returned to the Black Forest to perfect his jousting," said the Baron. "Still think Harold is the man to run the military, do you?"

"Once I'm crowned king then Harold will run the military. There's none better!" answered Tostig.

"Of course, since Edward the Confessor has no heirs, we don't know who will be crowned king", responded Bishop Verser without looking up from penning the documents.

"That's undisputed! Tostig will be the next King of Angle land!" declared the Baron.

Tostig shifted in his chair and smiled derisively in the direction of the Bishop. "Bishop Verser likes nothing more than to play the gravely serious and wise old sage, always willing to lay a profound egg here and there--but really, what is he, but a wily provocateur?"

The Bishop smiled and shook his head, but never looked up at Tostig while penning the documents.

Bishop Verser was a great observer of nature. He felt that all mysteries of the universe could ultimately be answered by the natural world, which he felt was the ultimate expression of his god.

In his youth Bishop Verser had made an interesting experiment; he had observed that one kind of duck flew over grain fields for food, and another kind of duck swam in ponds and dived for fish. He bred the two different ducks, because he was curious about the behavior of the offspring. Once the eggs hatched he watched them and took notes as they matured. An odd thing occurred; the ducks had *inherited the urge to dive for their food, but not the ability,* so they spent their entire life thrusting their head underwater until they nearly drowned, and then they would pop their head up again. They would repeat this behavior over and over, because they had no control over this demonic urge. It was, perhaps, the most unfortunate hereditary behavior that he had ever witnessed.

But the Bishop also observed that there were human beings that were "diving ducks", like Tostig, for example. Tostig, observed the bishop, had inherited *'the urge to rule – but not the ability'.* He was a 'diving duck'. Tostig, he felt, was indeed subject to a hereditary disorder that he had no control over – and yet he was in line to be King of Angle Land. This gave the Bishop pause -- a diving duck sitting on the throne? God have mercy on us!

After a while he laid down the quill and stared out the arched window across the wide fields and rolling hills of Wessex, and beyond the horizon where Harold Godwinson lay very still in Normandy.

CHAPTER X

Adelize, Harold, and the Green Knight

NORMANDY WAS UNDER SIEGE BY the same storm and driving rain as Wessex. The windows were locked tight, the doors were shut, yet drafts in William's castle still flew the curtains and threatened to extinguish the many candles and torches that were lit in Harold's room. He was bathed in perspiration, and he alternated between sleep and delirium. A weary Adelize assisted the doctor in removing leeches from his neck and chest. William leaned over and lifted the blanket on Harold, screwing up his face as he examined the deep wound. The doctor shook his head and gravely reiterated his earlier prognosis. "There's no other way, William. You can see that it's beginning to rot." William nodded and began tying Harold down. After a moment he demanded that Adelize leave the room. Adelize knew that this was not the time to be headstrong. She left the room and stood in the hallway. After a while she dropped to her knees, bowed her head, crossed herself and prayed for the first time since Harold was injured in Brittany.

A white hot iron was removed from the oven of the blacksmith and quickly carried across the yard, into the castle, up the stairs, down the hallway, past a praying Adelize, and into Harold's room. William took the hot iron and laid it against the infected area of Harold's wound. There was a terrible scream that came from the dark castle and spilled into the surrounding forests, and then all was quiet.

Days later Adelize walked into Harold's candle-lit room carrying a bowl of water and a towel. She gently placed the bowl on a table, lit two more candles, and then undressed. After wetting the towel in the bowl she slid naked under the blankets and daubed his perspiring face, pausing from time to time to brush the reddish hair streaked with dark auburn from his forehead, intermittently showering his face with tiny kisses, and whispering quietly to him. She stared at him in adulation, fascinated with his breathing in and breathing out. After a while she fell asleep with her right ear lying on his chest, listening to the sound of his heart.

In the earliest morning light Adelize stirred, and then woke with a start, realizing that Harold was no longer next to her. In a near panic she scanned the room, finally seeing Harold lying on the floor near the balcony. She moved quickly to Harold, who was shiny with perspiration and barely conscious. She slid her hands underneath his head and raised it from the floor. Harold half opened his eyes and asked this question:

"Did I win?"

Harold thought that he was still at the Brittany joust. Adelize was so happy that she began crying.

Mother Nature looked as though she were laying down for her winter rest....

It was autumn in Normandy, and the afternoon was sunny, quiet, and uncharacteristically warm. The shadows were long in the middle of the day, and the trees, most of them, were already bare. Mother Nature looked as though she were laying down for her winter rest, but somehow found that she was unable to fall asleep, so she simply laid there and allowed the remaining warmth of the season to slowly sedate her until autumn finally faded away.

Harold and Adelize were on the front lawn of the castle. Adelize was sewing up Harold's wound with a needle and thread. Harold was shirtless, seated, and staring off into the distance. He was watching a couple of ravens torment a hawk, who would from time to time do a roll over and threaten the ravens with his talons, but the ravens were always one step ahead of the hawk and laughed their way out of it.

Harold was growing impatient with Adelize's sewing and kept asking how much longer. She tried to explain that this was scar tissue, and that was why it kept tearing open. She was in the process of explaining for the twentieth time that he could not resume normal activities, like jousting and fighting, until this healed properly, but she was interrupted.

"Who is this riding towards us, Adelize?" Adelize stared at the distant rider and safely concluded that it was The Green Knight.

"I don't' like him, Harold," she said.

"Why?"

"He's insulting and abrasive. I heard what he called you. He called you a 'choir boy'."

Harold began to tense up. "Well, if he wants to challenge me, he'll have to wait until I get dressed."

"You're not doing anything! My father won't let you!"

Harold turned to her, and seeing that she was serious -- burst out laughing, which provoked a laugh with Adelize. Wondering if he heard her right, he asked "Your father won't let me, Adelize? Did you really say that?" Harold laughed again. "You're making me pop a stitch, Adelize. Now stop it!" he said, while holding on to his side.

The Green Knight approached, lowered his lance and removed his helmet.

"Good day, my lady! Good day, sir!" Adelize coldly glanced up at him and then resumed sewing.

"Good day!" said Harold.

"That's a nasty wound!" observed the Green Knight. Harold nodded.

"I'm returning to Scotland," announced the Green Knight.

"Scotland? I thought that you were from Paris," replied Harold.

"I fought there for four years, but Scotland is my home." And after a deeply internalized moment the Green Knight continued, "Before I left Normandy I wanted to tell you that I am sure that it was you that I saw fight nameless at the Winchester tournament – at that time you bore the shield of the Questing Beast. True?"

Harold hesitated, and then quietly said, "Aye! The shield was that of the Questing Beast."

"I know who you are, and I know you are a man of your people. I am here to pledge my fealty to your cause from this moment on, Black Knight."

Harold gently stopped Adelize's hand from sewing. He stood and walked to the Green Knight and held out his right hand.

"I am honored, Green Knight! Here is my hand, and my pledge." They clasped hands. "Comrades in arms, Black Knight!"

"Comrades in arms," repeated Harold, "And please give Malcolm my best!"

The Green Knight's face smiled, while his eyes in inverse proportion, grew sad. "I'm sorry, Harold, I can't do that."

Harold studied him before asking, "And why not, sir, if I may ask?"

After a quiet moment of looking into the soul of Harold and seeing a man that he felt he could trust the Green Knight answered, "My father was MacBeth." This caught Harold off guard.

"Then you are LuLach of Lanarkshire!?"

"Aye!" He nodded and looked away. After a time he turned back to Harold. "It hasn't been easy be-ing away from Scotland. I am a Scot, with the blood of the Highlander. We Scots grew out of the ground, exactly like the trees, the grass, the flowers, and the wildlife; and like the rivers and streams, our blood has coursed down the mountains and through the valleys since the beginning of time. I love the cold, the mist, the ancient megaliths, the bag pipes, the songs, the poetry, and the most beautiful faces of any people that God has ever put on this earth." And after a quiet moment, looking at a place far beyond the horizon, the Green Knight softly said, "But most of all…I miss my son…little Malory. In a word, I am homesick." The Green Knight turned to Harold and said, "My travels have taught me that I would rather be in a dungeon in the land of my ancestry than a free man in Paris." The Green Knight raised his lance and said, "Fare thee well, Black Knight!"

"Fare thee well, LuLach! And know that you will always have a home in the Land of the Angles."

The Green Knight nodded, and bidding Adelize farewell he turned his destrier and rode in the direction of the channel at an easy lope.

Adelize and Harold stood motionless for some time before Adelize asked, "His father was King of Scotland?" Harold nodded, and after a moment, while still watching the Green Knight as he rode up a distant hill, said "His father was overthrown and killed eight years ago – by Malcolm. And now MacBeth's son, LuLach, is living in exile, traveling and fighting in anonymity."

"Two minutes ago I had nothing but disdain for him, but now my heart breaks for him," said Adelize.

"Why?"

"Because he is separated from all that he finds worthwhile in this life – and now he is talking about ending his life by returning to Scotland, and that's certainly what will happen if he goes back. What do you think?"

"I think that what you have so well described is exactly why he is the Green Knight," said Harold.

"How do you mean?"

"He is like the moth that circles the flame, attracted by the light and at the same time repelled by the heat -- and after a time grows weary, and so he flies directly into it."

"But that's... tragic! I'm thinking that maybe we should coax him not to return to Scotland."

"That's like telling a bird not to fly, Adelize."

"You seem to be really sure of yourself on this subject. How do you know this?"

"Because he's a brother." Harold smiled, and then turned away from her.

After a while Adelize smiled and said, "Well, sit down, Black Knight, and let me finish my work." She began sewing again. "You can't feel me sewing?" she asked, but Harold was preoccupied with several flowers next to the bench that they were sitting on.

"What do you call this wildflower?" He leaned over and picked one of them and twirled it under his nose.

"That is what we call 'fleur de lis' which is a type of iris that grows wild around here. Why?"

"They're beautiful!"

"They're abundant here. You don't have any in Angle Land?"

"No. But we will. I'm taking some home and planting them. And I will also change their name."

"What will you call them on the island?"

"I shall call them...'Sweet Adelize'."

It's rare for Adelize to blush, but blush she did. She hid her face from Harold while continuing her sewing. "I'll hold you to it," she said.

"You won't have to," said Harold, who had become preoccupied with a distant rider. "Adelize, who is that talking with the Green Knight?" Adelize replied without looking, "That's my father, bidding the Green Knight farewell."

"How do you know if you don't look up?"

"I always know when my father is around. He has a very strong presence, don't you think?"

Harold weighed the words of Adelize, and then nodded in agreement. "The strongest of any man I've ever known."

"Really?" and after a thoughtful moment added, "You're the first one...that he has ever liked."

"The first one....? I'm the first person that he has ever liked?" he asked, turning to her with a smile. Adelize had slipped, and was slightly embarrassed. "No, Harold. You're the first one that he has liked... that I have..." She broke off, flustered. "He likes you... leave it at that!" she said, with a child-like giggle.

"I'm glad," said Harold, adding after a moment, "Or maybe the word is 'relieved'."

She smiled. "He's really very sweet, you know...unless you're in his way, then he's not so sweet."

Harold chuckled, nodded in agreement, and then turned to her. "I'll miss you, Adelize."

"No you won't."

"I won't?"

"No! Because I'm coming to Angle Land to visit you.... and if there's a woman there, I'll toss her off the balcony --- swan neck and all!"

Harold began laughing. "Stop making me laugh! It hurts my stitches." After a quiet moment Harold said to her with a smile,

"Yes Adelize, you're the daughter of William. There can be no doubt!"

Adelize knotted the thread and made her final loops.

"There! All done!"

CHAPTER XI

The Duke and the Earl: An

interesting proposal

WILLIAM RODE UP WITH AN ancient hunter whose name was Fletcher. William nodded and dismounted.

"Adelize darling, your mother wants to see you-- and I'd like to have a few words with Harold in private."

Adelize knew exactly when to resist her father – and when not to resist. By his tone Adelize knew that now was not the time to resist. She climbed on her horse, said her goodbyes with a smile, and rode away.

William looked at Harold's new stitches. "Nasty wound. It makes my legs hurt just to look at it."

Harold, noticing that William's arm was no longer swollen, commented on the rapid healing. William explained that he had utilized the bark from the willow trees in Brittany, as the druids had suggested, and said that he had sat in the hot mineral baths there, following their explicit mandate. Within a short time in the hot baths his swollen arm continued to swell and was ready to burst, until the chief druid poked holes into it with a hunting knife: It drained copiously through these holes for hours, said William, until his arm returned to a near-normal size. After that it healed fast, and within a matter of days was no longer painful. William suggested to Harold that he visit Konan's druids in Brittany to treat his injury before returning, and if he did so he should return with some seeds from those peculiar willow trees to take back to Angle Land with him.

William introduced Harold to Fletcher as the engineer who had designed the bows and arrows for his military, and added that Fletcher had designed a new modification with a unique composite of several woods that he was eager to demonstrate. Fletcher pulled a huge bow from his horse and stood it on the ground. It was taller than most men.

"That is the longest bow that I've ever seen, William. What's it made from…the yew tree?"

"That, and others! Would you like to try it?"

"I'd pop a stitch," said Harold.

"My arm has not fully recovered. Go ahead, Fletcher!"

Fletcher strung the bow, and though in his twilight years pulled the bow with the unusually long arrow to its full length.

"Now watch where the arrow lands and mark the distance," said William enthusiastically.

Fletcher let the arrow fly. The arrow soared, soared, and soared, and finally landed, in Harold's estimation, over two hundred and fifty meters away in a most idyllic spot on a lower cliff overlooking all the land.

William beamed. "Have you ever seen such distance?"

Harold agreed that he had never seen an arrow fly so fast and so far. William confided that he was having several hundred of the longbows made up right away, and after referring to the spot that the arrow had landed turned to Harold and told him that he was going to build a castle on that beautiful location, and that the castle would be for Harold and Adelize.

Harold smiled, and was uncharacteristically at a loss for words. William saw Harold's hesitation and sought to comfort him by telling him not to worry about Adelize's age; that he and Matilda were married when they were very young. Harold was speechless and continued to nod and smile. William went on, telling Harold that it was no secret that he and Adelize were very fond of one another, and then sought to conclude things with this final piece of relevant information: "Let me tell you something else, Harold. Matilda is a direct descendent of Alfred the Great. How would you like to have the blood of Alfred flowing through the veins of those fine sons that you will have?"

"I admire no man in all of Anglish history more than Sir Alfred," said Harold.

William turned to Harold and looked deep within his soul. Harold felt the hair on his arm stand on end. William's eyes were like a wild storm in the night, though his voice and manner were steady and calm. Harold could see that William's entire nature, and all that he was about in this life, had consolidated into a distinct agenda, and he had a feeling that he was about to be apprised of exactly what that agenda was at this very moment.

"I am with you on that, Harold. Alfred was a great man. If he were here today, I think that he would agree that the blood and the culture of the Angles and the North Man should be bound together for all eternity. This alliance would prove to be the strongest in all of Europe – and you would be my number one man, Harold."

"This is too generous, William. You overrate my position -- and my abilities."

"I don't overrate you, Harold. You simply underrate yourself. You are a man of great leadership ability," and following these words, William, in a show of conviction clasped Harold firmly by each shoulder with his powerful hands and leaned into him; Harold watched as William's eyes danced in his head,

"Mark what I say, Harold! I am William the Conqueror! I can see into the hearts of men like no man walking this earth."

Harold nodded and told William that he was overwhelmed and at a loss for words. William continued, telling Harold that tomorrow night there would be a farewell banquet for him, and that he would let him tell Adelize the news in his own time. Harold had no sooner thanked William for this when two ravens flew past uncharacteristically close on Harold's right. He knew this to be a Norse omen of some kind, but he wasn't exactly sure as to what it meant.

William mounted his horse. Fletcher, already mounted, waved to Harold as he and William rode away.

CHAPTER XII

The Covenant over Bones of Saints

THE SUN HAD JUST SET, and Harold, from an elevated balcony on the top of the castle, watched as a couple of distant ravens flew above trees that were leafless and bare. They were through stirring up trouble for the day, and were looking for a choice place to roost. He turned back to the bustling crowd below. He was deliberating about the extraordinary amount of guards and military personnel mulling around when he heard Matilda's soft voice behind him.

He turned to see the beautiful lady, who had already lost the revitalization of her spirit that had soared so high on the day of the Brittany tournaments. Her angst had returned, and had driven out that day's sparkle and bliss. This bothered Harold, but he dared not allow his feelings about this to be gauged by anybody, including her.

"Good evening, Harold!" said Matilda. She shivered slightly and clasped her hands around her body.

"Good evening, Matilda! I am wondering why there are so many guards and military personnel here tonight. What is the occasion?"

"It's simply William's way of showing you his gratitude and respect." Harold was a man utterly devoid of guile and craft, and consequently never suspected guile and craft in others. With an innocent smile, he observed: "Well, if this has to do with me, then it's quite a farewell gathering -- and I'm honored."

After a difficult moment Matilda stepped close to Harold, and dropping her voice she spoke with a deep urgency. "Harold, you must allow yourself to be viewed as an ally tonight."

"Ally to what?"

At that moment an envoy rounded the corner some distance away led by LanFranc's man in Normandy, Mortaine.

Matilda continued in a barely audible whisper, "To the most insatiable appetite for conquest since Caesar and Alexander!"

The Parisian Mortaine stepped forward, greeted Matilda with a deep bow, and turned to Harold with a practiced smile. With an obsequious tilt of the head, Mortaine inquired as to the state of Harold's injury from the Brittany joust. The two men made small talk, and then Mortaine motioned Harold to follow him into the castle.

Harold found himself being escorted down the long castle hallway, lit by torches on both sides, with guards on his left, guards on his right, to his front, and to the rear. Harold found that there was a persistent and stubborn question that kept elbowing its way to the surface until finally it emerged from the fog of his soul and refused to leave until it received an answer. "Harold, are you a guest...or a prisoner?"

The audibility of the choir voices intensified. They paused at the doorway. The guards swung open the huge doors and revealed the Duke's council chamber. The majestically huge chamber was filled with most of the major figures of Normandy. Sitting amongst them on an elevated throne was William. The air swirled with pageantry of all sorts. Torches lit the background, candles lit the foreground, and as Harold stepped forward the singing voices swelled to a crescendo. Symbols of nation, religion, and heritage were seen everywhere.

In front of William was a sacred golden cloth that had been carefully rolled up and placed in the center of a table. On the left and on the right were strange black hooded crones, whose faces could not be seen. William, still sitting, barely moved his hand and the singing ceased. The entire Commune Concilium bowed deeply in what had to be Harold's honor. William stood and took several steps down to greet Harold; but instead of addressing him directly, he turned to the left, and then to the right saying, "We of the Commune Concilium of Normandy honor our brother, Harold of Angle Land."

Each time William finished a sentence there was a pause, filled by liturgical acclamations by the counsel. "And on this day we gather here to wish him a safe and speedy return to his native country, and to exchange the oaths of homage, and to further deepen and consecrate these most sacred of vows."

With a nod of the head the black hooded crones moved forward and undid the band that tied the golden cloth. The cloth was spread; revealing the various bones of what were unquestionably several humans; later to be described as the bones of ancient saints. A nervous and confused Harold listened as William continued, "To redeliver our previous words, Harold of Angle Land, do you love and honor Adelize, and if so, will you consent to marry her?"

Harold glanced about in confusion. "I do love and honor Adelize, and I would marry her—if only she would have me." There were mutterings among the crones.

And now William continued, slowing down his tempo, slightly raising his voice, and annunciating every syllable perfectly,

"And will you assist me, Harold, in securing my right as the only living blood heir to the Anglish throne, and in so doing, forge a common destiny between the Land of the Angles and the Land of the North Man?"

Harold saw the trap and began to perspire. After a silence that had become increasingly tense, Harold said these words: "To redeliver our previous words, William, I will do what is right, for I can always be counted on to follow the dictates of my conscience."

There was a moment of silence, and then came the sounds of the council turning in their seats to examine William, to see how he would reply to Harold's ambivalence. William hesitated on this answer, but skillfully turned it to his advantage.

"The very words that we had hoped for, Harold! Now, dauntless knight, pray...give me your hand."

Harold took a step forward. Over the bones of the golden cloth William extended his hand, and Harold accepted. They clasped hands.

"Over these bones of the ancient Saints of Normandy – "The ecclesiastics crossed themselves and uttered over and over, "Super sanctimus reliquas...super santimus reliquas..." as William continued "The common destiny of the Norse Land, and the Land of the Angles has been forged over the bones of the sacred saints, and may violation of our now sealed enterprise bring down the vengeance of Cherniborg, the black devil..." The members of the Concilium crossed themselves, and continued in a heightened manner uttering, "Super sanctimus reliquas". William clasped Harold's hands with both of his, and looking Harold straight in the eye announced for all in the chamber to hear, "Brothers forever!"

Harold repeated, "Brothers forever!" William turned to the Concilium and announced, "Then it is sealed!"

The choir voices burst forth with a dazzling energy that surged against the cathedral ceiling, and all turned to one another with smiles and handshakes. European history of the highest order had been made.

CHAPTER XIII

Princess Adelize and her

Dauntless Knight

LATER THAT NIGHT HAROLD SAT with his face buried in his hands on a balcony of the castle that overlooked the shining moonlit river. The river seemed to be only as far from the castle as one of Fletcher's arrow flights; he would be on that river tomorrow, headed for the coast of Normandy.

He tried to mentally recreate the vows that he had made earlier, wondering if he had just given away Angle Land, or at least if he had given that impression. It was clear to him that they had the will to interpret everything that was said and done to their end, and that was the whole story. He had no witnesses to support him. Not a one. He no longer wondered if he and William were friends. After tonight he concluded that a man like William doesn't really have friends; he only has people that serve his obsession – and that was a harsh truth that he would have to learn to accept. Yet, in spite of that realization, he considered William a friend -- a friend of a special kind -- for there had never been a William, and there probably would never be another. There was only one.

As he sat gazing at the river that reflected the intense light of a three quarter moon, Matilda's words returned to him "...the most insatiable appetite for conquest since Caesar and Alexander!"

Ultimately, for those who were obsessed by conquest, like William, Caesar, and Alexander, there was not a single thing in their lives that could be considered 'real', except their enemies. This explained why William was at war continuously; and this was exactly why Harold had gone down a different path in life than the rest of his family. He, up to now, had succeeded in staying away from the world of artificial handshakes and smiles. Yes, thinking on it, the Green Knight was a true brother who understood these things, and had managed to avoid these strangling predicaments that Harold now found himself in; and he had avoided them by traveling nameless and living on the outside.

He thought of Adelize; she was a royal wildflower who had brought him a joy that he had never known before. She was everything a person should be. To him she had been a gift, and had never failed to stir up the best part of him, unlike Edith-of-the-Swan's-Neck, who had a gift for bringing out the devil in him.

Harold reached down and picked up a potted "fleur de Lis'", as Adelize had described them. He twirled it under his nose. The scent of the iris was, like Adelize, thoroughly intoxicating.

"Sweet Adelize", he said. He had just pulled a blanket around his shoulders and was staring out across the moonlit river when he heard a reply,

"Yes, dauntless knight!"

Harold reacted with a start, staring in the direction of the voice, yet seeing nothing. He went to the rail of the castle balcony, and there she was – smiling, beautiful, and completely out of her mind! She had climbed a wooden trellis straight up from the castle grounds and was hovering a good forty feet in the air. Harold, who had great difficulty with heights, had a hard time just looking over the rail of the castle balcony.

"Have you lost your mind? What's wrong with you? Get over here!"

Adelize smiled sweetly and asked Harold to give her his hand. Harold took her hand and started to help her over the short wall and onto the balcony, but she stopped him.

"Your hand is trembling. Why?"

"I don't know that my hand is trembling."

"It is. I heard that you made a promise to marry me tonight. Is that why your hands are trembling, because you didn't mean it?"

"No Adelize, of course not!"

"Did you mean it when you said that you loved me?"

"Yes, Adelize, from my heart's core, I meant it. Now get up here!"

"Then you must say it to me, Harold, and not just to the Commune Concilium."

"I will. Now climb up here, Adelize, and we'll talk about it."

"No."

What do you mean, "No"?

"I mean that I'm getting dizzy."

"What?"

"I think I'm going to fall."

"You're being absurd!"

"And then you'll never get back to the island. Try explaining my dead body at the bottom of this trellis to my father."

"Alright Adelize, you have to stop this madness right now!"

"Kiss me!"

Harold looked at her for a short while and then leaned down and kissed her for some time.

"Do you love me?"

"I used to -- five minutes ago, until you started this nonsense. Yes, of course I love you Adelize. I love you with all of my heart."

"And these deliverances aren't made under duress?"

"Adelize, you are so much like your father that it's uncanny. Now please just get off the trellis and climb over the balcony!"

Adelize climbed over the short wall and onto the balcony. Harold firmly clasped her by the shoulders and looked directly into her eyes with his own, which were blazing in his head like a wild fire. "Adelize, promise me that you will never do anything like that again – ever -- for the rest of your life!"

Adelize threw back her head and laughed, and what a clarion laugh it was. "Oh dauntless knight, my brothers and I have climbed that trellis a hundred times."

Adelize sat down on a bench and tossed her lengthy blonde hair out of her eyes. She crossed her long lean legs while smiling up at Harold. The moonlight lit her deep blue green eyes, and accentuated the pout of her lips. She gave Harold a serious look, and then tossed it away with another full laugh that echoed off the castle walls and spilled out into the courtyard. She patted the seat next to her while smiling.

"Please sit next to me."

Harold, who still had not recovered from the trellis prank, slowly sat down next to the unpredictable Adelize. "There is only one," he said to himself.

She placed her hand on his forehead. "Your forehead is damp, and your hand is still trembling. What kind of farewell party was that, that would daunt my dauntless knight?

"An unforgettable one!" he answered.

"I've thought about something all day, Harold... something that the Green Knight said...he said that on your shield was a figure of the Questing Beast."

"Yes."

"And he said that he knew your cause. Was it because of the sign of the Questing Beast?"

"Yes!"

"And what is the Questing Beast?"

Harold began removing a pendant from around his neck while he answered her.

"It's a legendary animal who lives in Wales--it looks like this."

The Questing Beast

Harold handed her the pendant. She took it and examined it under the moonlight. It had the chimaerean figure of the Questing Beast. She continued to scrutinize it while wanting to know, "What cause could it represent?"

"Truth; honor; courage; courtesy; respect for women; and dignity for all men!"

"And the Green Knight?"

"There's an order of knights that pursues the best in man, although, like the Questing Beast, it can never be fully conquered. It's a brotherhood. The Green Knight is one of those knights."

Harold took the pendant from Adelize's hand and slowly put it around her neck.

"It's yours." They leaned forward and kissed. After a moment he said to her, "Now it's you that is trembling. Why?"

"Because you're leaving tomorrow."

And again they kissed, which rapidly erupted into a burning fever.

CHAPTER XIV

The Return of Harold

OFF THE NORMAN COAST A Viking square-rigger cut the channel waves. A south wind billowed the white sail with gold trim, while Matilda's Captain Airard shouted commands in Flemish to the few crew members.

Harold stood near the stern, his eyes riveted on a tiny figure dressed in all white that was waving from a distant hill that overlooked the coast. It was Adelize. He waved back once again. It was an image of her that he would hold in his heart for the rest of his life.

Captain Airard stepped next to Harold, and over the din of the hull crashing through the waves said, "It's a brisk wind, Harold. We should see the river Thames by noon – perhaps before!" Harold nodded, but remained riveted on a distant Adelize.

The Captain, with a smile of great warmth, said "Sir, we are now far enough into the channel that, in accordance with the wishes of Princess Adelize, please allow me to grace you with a small surprise."

The Captain motioned with his head. Harold turned and followed the Captain, watching him as he nodded to his son, Stephen, to remove a large square-rigger sail that had been folded over and used as a cover on the deck to conceal something. Stephen complied with the captain's wishes and with the aid of another crew member rolled back the sail, revealing in the neighborhood of eight dozen potted plants of the wild Norman iris, known by them as the fleur d lis'.

Harold was overcome with emotion and stood transfixed. Stephen unfolded another sail and revealed several caged white carrier pigeons with a note attached to one of the cages. The captain smiled while buttoning up his coat. Harold bent down and took the note from the cage. The note read:

Now that you're out of sight,
Before day meets night,
Let your words take flight,
And write, Dauntless Knight!

Harold smiled and looked up. His eyes searched the horizon for the tall blonde headed girl dressed in all white who had stood waving with her heart in her hand. She was no longer there.

———◆———

From the chateau de' Falaise Matilda released a white pigeon. It soared high above the Normandy landscape, darting to the left and to the right, disoriented and confused; but suddenly, by some unknown and highly mysterious internal mechanism it turned west. After that there was no searching for direction – it flew straight as one of Fletcher's arrows to an abbey in Sussex.

On the roof of this abbey were several cages of pigeons; and tending these pigeons was a freckle-faced adolescent boy with intense green eyes and protruding upper teeth; teeth which could be seen even when his lips were at rest. He was the apparent caretaker of these birds. The Falaise pigeon landed on a sill next to the young boy. The boy noticed that it had a note attached, and so he moved carefully towards it.

He gently picked up the bird and removed the note. With great care he placed the bird in a pen with his brothers and sisters, and though they had never met one another, they greeted each other with sobs and coos, and inquired about the journey, the speed of the wind, the source of the journey, and whether or not there had been a hawk-sighting, and on and on, while the young boy busied himself trying to make sense out of the note.

The note was written in an unfamiliar style, so the boy knew that it had to contain a weighty matter of some kind. He ran down the stairs, hitting every other step, and when in the hallway he burst into a bare-footed sprint. A moment later he arrived at the room of a monk, who had been carefully penning a document. The monk took the note and read it carefully several times. The boy noted that the monk was, while reading the note, nodding his head and making sounds that were very similar to his pigeons on the roof when they were being fed.

"It's from Normandy, and it says, 'Harold of Essex arrives in London this afternoon on a dragon boat'."

A caped rider exploded from the abbey doors and was already at full speed before he reached the end of the drawbridge. The rider turned north, and with the sun on his back navigated the winding dusty road through the dark forest at a full gallop.

Within the massive halls of Westminster Abbey were a flood of torches and candles that lit the normally dark interior. The sound of a harp gently cascaded from an upper balcony, and everywhere were seen hooded figures that were quietly praying. The king of twenty-three years, Edward the Confessor, son of Aethelred the Unready, was sinking away. Each moment, to those in attendance, seemed to be the king's last. From time to time his eyes would slowly shut, and those nearby would think to themselves, "There he goes." But then after a while his eyes would open again. "What the devil is keeping him alive?" they would ask themselves, and then they became somewhat ashamed for allowing such a question to emerge from the fog of their consciousness; but once they crossed themselves several times then things were put back to normal.

Sitting next to King Edward was the honorable Bishop Verser. Bishop Verser had delivered the urgent message regarding Harold's arrival. After a while the king's eyes opened, as though rising from the dead. He motioned for the Bishop to lean in so that the Bishop could hear what was being said, since Edward was apparently not capable of speaking above a low whisper.

"Thank our wonderful lord in heaven," he said. "Please bring Harold to me now, Bishop! I want you to go personally. Send no one else!"

———◆———

Harold waved goodbye to Captain Airard and his son Stephen as the captain navigated the dragon boat toward the estuary of the River Thames. Harold was dressed in a non-descript wear that would not in any way reveal to others that he was one of the most powerful men in Angle Land. To dress as a commoner was a fondness of his. He found that when he did this those around him did not force laughs, and fawn and scrape each time he barely moved his head or his hand. That kind of artificial behavior he considered a gross nuisance. He understood the reason for it, but still, he didn't like it. It was far more interesting for him to listen to the lives of his fellow countrymen when they were being genuine about the affairs of state, or even railed against the ruling royalty. It was these men that would openly tell you where the hole was that the devil crawls out of at night, where the best poaching spots were, where Odin was now living, who built Stonehenge, whether or not the king had spies in people's homes, and whether or not the ships that did not return from the sea were devoured by sea monsters the size of the Westminster Abbey, and on and on.

And then there were times around the campfires, while disguised as a common soldier, that he would hear thoughts so profound from some of these men that he was in a sense startled by them, and he found himself wandering in the night harboring a certain awe for the common man. In short, he would gain a look at a cross-section of his people and his land that royalty had almost always intentionally isolated themselves from and knew absolutely nothing about – and by doing so the rule makers had become, in many ways, entirely irrelevant and useless.

Of course Harold found himself being the punch-line of many jokes because of this strange trait, but that was perfectly alright with him. "He is an odd one!" they would say. "Thank god I'm an odd one," he would quietly say to himself, while taking a look around at the members of the court – the witnamagote, as it was called. From early on he chose to distance himself from the gait and manner of the dandified fops of royalty, which he had absolutely no intention of snuggling up to.

Harold was a man that was known to have a preference for sleeping on the ground in the rain – rather than a feather bed in a castle – if it meant that he was going to be in the company of people who were, like himself, incapable of lying. Yes, Harold Godwinson was a strange man. His reputation became even more acute when asked at a ceremony for graduating knights, in the event of his death on the battlefield, how he would like to be remembered by others. Without hesitating Harold said,

"I would like to be known – and remembered -- as the man that could not be bought."

After that many speculated that Harold could very well have been dropped on his head as a baby. That was the explanation that made the most sense to those compatriots that never grew tired of delving into the subject of the strangeness of Harold Godwinson.

On this day Harold, after watching the captain safely navigate the estuary in the dragon boat, turned to a man who was along in his years. He was a geezer, and a crusty one at that. The crusty geezer had signaled his impatience by clearing his throat several times. He had long ago loaded up the potted plants and the pigeons on the small cart, pulled by a horse that was also along in its years, and was also impatient; both the horse and the geezer had been sighing out loud to catch Harold's attention -- but it didn't work. Harold's gaze could not be bent until he was sure that the captain was safely bound for the return trip to Normandy.

After the captain was out of sight Harold turned to the impatient man and asked a question as a small tor-ment, "Well, are you *finally* ready, sir?" without a hint of a smile.

The geezer flew into a minor rage that Harold thought was completely entertaining. The man was of the Welsh stock that had somehow ended up near London. His first language was the same as the Green Knight and Konan's; it was Keltic; better known by some as "Gaelic". The man was descended from those who fought the Germanic tribes from the north for a hun-dred and fifty years, and after their hero, King Arthur was killed, they were then driven back to the western shores of Angle Land to an area known as Wales. They were a tough and saucy breed, but prone to wild exag-gerations and hot tempers, as Caesar described them in his writings.

The Welshman that Harold would be traveling with, seemed to Harold, to personify this strain of Keltic temperament. At the moment the he was en-raptured by the legend of Stonehenge, so he did not have a problem with schooling Harold about this mys-terious structure on the plains of Salisbury. The old man, who was seated on the cart while Harold walked next to him, became more and more excited, with his eyes bulging out of his head and saliva flying from his mouth on every syllable.

"Any fool can see that it would take a race of giants to build that Stonehenge. But where did they go? Are they sleeping in a cave somewheres? And what did they eat?"

As the man was talking Harold would bend over from time to time and dislodge a large stone in the ground, leaving a perfectly sized hole to put the potted iris plant in. In the meantime he answered the crusty geezer's question, "The giants probably ate each other, and that's why there are no giants left."

"Nay," said the geezer. "There would be one giant left!"

"Well, then he should be very hungry by now," mused Harold, while carefully covering the roots of the iris with soil.

"Not so, Sire! He'll eat a horse in a single gulp. This land, you see, used to be thick with horses. Now take a look!"

Harold took a look around. He nodded and concluded that there weren't many horses in sight – in fact, there was only one that he could see.

"There's your proof!" and with that, the Welshman was well satisfied that the door had been forever closed on the subject of Stonehenge. He continued with some fascination to watch Harold plant the flowers along the way, and finally had to ask, "Who be your master, Sire?"

"My master?" asked Harold.

"Aye, lad! Whose flowers and birds are these, anyway, and why are ye planting them?" queried the geezer.

"These flowers and birds belong to Harold, Earl of Essex."

At this moment he became wide-eyed and stopped his horse. This single act alone signified a matter of crushing importance.

"Criminy! Why your master is dead, Sire. He drowned in the channel -- some time ago, it was."

"Are you sure?" asked Harold, with unwavering earnest.

"Aye!", said the geezer, and as he continued his eyes bulged as much any frog that Harold had ever seen in his life.

"The wenchifier and carouser that he was--he fell off the boat while intertwined with a wench--in the fog-- drinking....!"

"Why that's a shame," replied Harold.

He studied Harold intently, and then gently asked, "You don't appear to be too upset, Sire. Did your master Harold...did he beat you? I am sorry if he did!"

Harold could no longer conceal a laugh.

"No! Not at all!"

"Now his brother, Tostig," observed the man, "will most certainly be our next king. King Edward's health is poor, and the unfortunate man has no blood heirs, Sire."

But Harold was staring at the road ahead.

"Who are the riders coming our way?"

A regiment of columned knights appeared, having rounded a curve in the forest.

"Criminy! It's the King's Knights! Quickly, get the cart over or we'll be trampled!"

Harold, standing next to the cart, raised his hand at the approaching knights, but the Bishop and the knights paid him no mind as they flew past.

Suddenly Bishop Verser held up his hand and slowed his horse to a stop. He turned his horse and stared in the direction of the cart. "That was Harold, for god's sake!" The knights snapped their horses around and took a hard look at the man dressed like a commoner. After a moment all charged back to see whether or not their favorite knight had survived the shipwreck in Normandy and had returned home after all. Seconds later there was a celebration with laughter and tears of joy.

Harold turned to see Bishop Verser, his most cherished and trusted friend. They clasped each other with a powerful hug that went on for some time. The bishop confided that Harold's presence was needed immediately, saying to him that Edward's life was balanced only by the hope that he would see Harold before he passed away.

The Sergeant jumped from his horse and handed Harold the reins. Harold climbed on the horse and told the sergeant, "Sergeant, have the knights escort this kind gentleman, along with my flowers and my birds, to the palace."

"It is my command, Sir."

Harold extended his hand to the Welshman, bidding him fare well, and telling him that he was invited to dine in the castle with him and the king's knights at their table this evening. He accepted the invitation with a nervous display of his remaining teeth and an involuntary jerk of the neck. Harold and the bishop, flanked on each side by knights, galloped away in a cloud of dust.

CHAPTER XV

Edward the Confessor: Kingmaker

WHEN HAROLD ENTERED THE MASSIVE torch-lit halls of Westminster Abbey all turned their heads in his direction. It was only a short time earlier that most had concluded that he was never to be seen again, so the mere sight of him was like seeing an apparition enter the great hallway.

On seeing Harold, King Edward raised his arms from his lying position.

Harold was profoundly moved by the man's poor condition. He sat next to Edward, and clasped the king's hands with his own. The king, to many, was apparently drawing on his final resources, for he showed more life when he sighted Harold then he had shown in a week. This did not escape those in attendance, which included all the major figures of Angle Land.

Harold was still dressed like a peasant, and his wound on his left side had reopened during the journey, so there was a large blood stain on the left side of his clothing. After a quiet moment King Edward asked,

"Jousting again, eh? I thought I told you to give that up."

"My lord, you may as well tell a bird not to fly," replied Harold.

There was muffled laughter in the large room. King Edward genuinely smiled through his illness.

Harold noticed that the man, whose complexion normally was pink, and when angered a deep maroon, now had become a lackluster gray. He had never seen Edward like this.

"It seems irresponsible to me. Who was the wench?" asked Tostig, who was sitting on the other side of the king.

"Now, now, Tostig...." admonished the king.

"His motives can always be traced to the same source," said Tostig, with his customary nasal whine.

"Hush now, Tostig!" And turning to Harold, asked "Now, Harold, that… wound. It happened in Normandy?

Harold nodded, and the king asked further if he had made the Duke of Normandy's acquaintance while in Normandy. Harold replied that he had.

"How did you get on with the Duke?"

"He's my good friend."

"Did he mention that my mother's brother was his grandfather?"

"He did."

"Ah, I knew it. And what else did he say?"

"He said that he felt that he should be King of Angle Land."

"Yes, I knew it. The Duke of Normandy, more than any man alive, is interested in my health--or rather, the failing of my health."

All in the massive room were craning their necks. They were astonished that Edward was showing this amount of life, when only moments earlier they had thought that he was irreversibly comatose and slipping into the afterlife.

After an intense breathing in and out, Edward turned to Tostig and said to him, while clutching his hand, "Tostig…"

Tostig, Harold's brother, on hearing his name moved slightly closer to Edward, screwing up his face in a possible effort to wring more tears, which he made no effort to wipe away.

"Yes, your Majesty?" and all in attendance noticed a piece of obvious theatre in Tostig's reply, as his voice slightly broke, as though overcome with a heartfelt emotion that he could not control.

Edward took Tostig's hand and held it gently while looking deeply into his eyes.

"You, Tostig, are the educated one in the family, refined and genteel, peaceful, understanding, and benevolent…like your father, my dearest friend, God bless him!"

"Yes. God bless him," repeated Tostig. "He was a wonderful, wonderful man, to be sure."

Edward let go of Tostig's hand and struggled to sit up in bed. When the others saw this they immediately assisted him, so that he could address, not just those close to him, but the entire witnamagote in the great torch lit hallway. As Edward begun, it was clear that he had been storing his resources for this final moment; for there was a resonance in his voice and a force in his manner not heard by those present for some time.

"Angle Land is beset with a peculiar problem. Our ancestors settled here, many of them, to escape Attila. The channel has provided our Angles, Saxons, Kelts, and Danes with a huge natural moat. But because it has insured their safety from the larger invasions, it has at the same time made our people fat and lazy. It's tragic, but most of our people don't even know that they are on an island."

During this Tostig was enthusiastically nodding in agreement on every point that Edward had made, and at one point he alone burst out in applause.

Edward glanced at him and then continued:

"Our people have no concept of nation--so if there is an invasion they will not act in concert, or as one, but only as a loose confederation of disjointed tribes. This I see as our glorious country's chief problem. It has to be rectified, Tostig."

Bristling with enthusiasm, Tostig drew closer, saying to Edward with a heartfelt sincerity, "Yes, it certainly does, your Majesty."

"This is why, after careful consideration and consultation, I have opted to have Harold succeed me as King of Angle Land."

There was a murmuring in the room. Tostig weaved slightly, his face lost color, his eyes became unfocused, and he reached for a rear bedpost for support, but missed, and would have hit the floor had it not been for an alert guard who caught him and propped him up.

"The crown is yours, Harold!" pronounced Edward, in a voice for all to hear so that there could be no disputes, debates, or re-examining matters later on. All were taken by surprise, none more than Harold. He started to speak but Edward talked over him.

"You have never seen yourself as a leader of men. Your perception of yourself is simply wrong. You are a great leader, and will be even greater, because it is you that will save this magnificent island from William." Edward paused for a moment, struggling to catch his breath before continuing,

"You will, like Alfred the Great, rule as the warrior-king, and repair all the damage that my rule has done to this fine land and wonderful people. In some ways, I must freely confess, I have been an absolutely wonderful king, and in some ways I have not. I am sorry to say that in my later years I have surrounded myself with far too many of these perfumed court dandies. We need less of those, and more warrior kings, like Alfred and Cnute. You are to drive the court dandies out into the fields where they shall be given hard work to re-align their judgments and bring them to their senses -- and then you must unite the far corners of our island. Ultimately you must strive to give to our people a sense of identity and national purpose. You are my choice, Harold, and Anglish Law gives me the right to choose my successor, above all other rights -- including the right of blood heirs. Now give me your hand!"

All were astonished. For those that knew him in his youth, this was the early Edward the Confessor, before he became soft and pliable. What happened here? What god had sent these Valkyries to boost his presence immeasurably in his final moments? All wondered as Harold accepted Edward's hand.

"Now give me your oath, Harold, and confirm to me that you will carry out the matters that we have discussed here today." After a time Harold said in a voice loud enough for all to hear, "I promise, your Majesty, to do my best to carry out your wishes."

"Then it is sealed!" proclaimed an exuberant Edward. Once he completed the sentence he laid back and fell into a deep sleep.

Hours later Harold lay on his back, watching dark clouds race past an icy January moon. He was lying on top of the roof of the Palace at Westminster, a place that he had been familiar with since early childhood. During his childhood he would hide from friends and family and, while lying on his back with his hands folded behind his head, stare at the starry sky while they searched for him. He could hear them calling around the woods, and the palace grounds, and throughout the castle, but he held fast, never budged, and never answered their calls. Harold felt that all people born on this earth were, during childhood, entitled to at least one secret hiding place – and this was his.

From here he could listen to the eerie call of the Tawny Owl from the forest, and watch their black silhouettes as they flew over the reflected silvery moonlight of the river Thames. The adult world used to tell Harold that these owl calls were actually ghosts of the beheaded criminals who were searching for their heads, and that's why their sounds were so unique and strange – because the bodies didn't have a mouth. But Harold knew better; he knew that this was a ruse concocted by adults to keep him from wandering around the palace grounds at night – but it didn't work. Harold had, by that time, become adept at having conversations with these owls, and his Tawny Owl call as a child was second to none, according to several of the old-timers.

Harold was, in fact, listening carefully to the call of a distant owl when he heard another sound nearby.

"Harold....Harold, I know that you're up there. Harold, please answer me!" After a moment Harold raised his head from the top of the castle wall and looked down the stairway. He recognized the voice immediately as Bishop Verser's. The bishop was the one person that Harold would allow to intrude on his privacy. Harold asked the bishop how he knew where to find him. The bishop, while catching his breath, answered that he remembered when Harold used to hide at this place from his father when he was a child.

"Besides Harold, I know what you're *really* doing up here!" added the bishop.

"Let's hear it, Bishop! What am I *really* doing up here?"

"You're up here gazing at the stars and wondering, hmmm....How can I fake my own death and then slip away to live in the Black Forest?"

Harold's hearty laugh resounded off the castle walls and rang through the stillness of the cold moonlit night. He sat up while shaking his head, his mood suddenly jocular.

"There is no privacy around you, Bishop. That's exactly what I was doing. You seem to know everything!"

Harold reached for his side, which only hurt when he laughed or coughed. The bishop pointed to a caged pigeon and asked, "Is this a new pet?" Harold explained that it was a carrier pigeon – a gift from a girl that he had met on the mainland, and after a lengthy pause confessed that he tried writing a note to her, but nothing seemed good enough.

The bishop replied only with a short nod, knowing that if he kept his mouth shut there would be more – and there was.

"I'm in love with her, Bishop Verser. She is the most perfect person I have ever met. She has a strange sense of humor, like me. We laugh at things that nobody else would ever think was humorous. And she makes me feel wonderful, when we all know that that is not the case. She is a blessing, bishop, but I don't know what to write to her. I have tried, but everything I think of seems…so senseless and inadequate. She's a poet, and I'm not!"

"You can always start by telling her that you're the new King of Angle Land. It has always had a measurable degree of success with women in the past."

"But I'm not the king yet?"

"You are the king, Harold. Edward left us a few moments ago. That's what I came to tell you."

"Edward is gone?"

"Edward is gone."

The bishop became concerned as he observed Harold, whose spirits seem to sink, rather than be elevated when he heard the news. After a time Harold confessed, "I haven't the pomp for this unsolicited

honor. Please advise me, Bishop!" The bishop could
see and hear a certain agony within Harold. The crown
was never his quest. To live outside the rules, like
the Green Knight, was how he saw himself traveling
through, as his Viking ancestors put it, "This tunnel of
light called life".

Now, suddenly, unsolicited, and in a bizarre twist of
fate, he not only was expected to follow the rules – he
was the rules.

The bishop placed his hand on Harold's shoulder
and looking him directly in the eye said, "Harold,
there is an old Viking saying that you have heard me
repeat before, and it goes like this:

'All you can do in this life is to try your best—the
outcome is none of your business'."

Harold laughed softly, and after nodding his head
for a while said, "I like that, Bishop Verser. Thank you
for reminding me of that!"

THE CORONATION OF HAROLD GODWINSON

On the sixth of January in the year 1066 in Westminster
Cathedral, all dukes, earls, barons, counts, prelates,
magistrates, and the ecclesiastic of Albion were pres-
ent. The choir sang "The Song of Ambrose" while
Harold kneeled at the altar. Bishop Verser prayed in
Latin for guidance by the spirit of wisdom. He prayed

for peace in the church, and for the best side of man's nature to prevail in the coming years.

The bishop asked for Harold to rise and face the crowd. After Harold stood, Bishop Verser, in the ancient tradition, asked the people gathered whether Harold should be crowned as Lord and King of Albion. The crowd by acclamation heartily assented – most of them. Harold's brother, Tostig, and a couple of his cronies stood with their arms folded.

While it was apparent to those who knew him best that Tostig was seething with jealousy, he was far too crafty for an open defiance.

At the bishop's prompting Harold made a solemn promise to his people:

"I hereby swear to all rights and liberties to which the glorious Edward had granted to his clergy and to his people, and to preserve peace to the church and God and all Anglish people, and to forbid wrongdoing to people of every realm, and to enforce justice and God's mercy in all judgments."

The choir raised its voices in the song, "Faith and Victory." Bishop Verser, in Latin, prayed that King Harold II may live forever. Harold, still kneeling, received the Insignia of the Holy Office. Bishop Verser continued in Latin and pronounced that Harold II should defend his land and smite the enemies of

Church and God. The Royal Sword was placed in Harold's hand, and the bishop continued:

"May the lord bless thee Harold II, who may for long years of life reign over a faithful people, in peace and concord, and if need be victory."

The people said "Amen." Harold turned to Bishop Verser and kneeled. Bishop Verser, while pronouncing the solemn words of ceremony anointed Harold with a small vile of holy oil.

"I do, in the name of our lord Jesus Christ, in the year of 1066 Anno Domini, now pronounce thee Harold Rex, King of the Angles, the Saxons, the Kelts, and the Danes -- of the Isle of Albion."

The Imperial Diadem of Britain was placed on Harold's head. The choir hit a crescendo with "Faith and Victory." Harold II stood and walked to the throne. He turned, bowed to the cheering crowd, and for the first time in his life he sat in a throne.

Harold II was handed the Royal Scepter, which he held above his head while the crowd continued to applaud wildly on its feet. Angle Land had a new king.

CHAPTER XVI

The Royal Banquet

IMMEDIATELY FOLLOWING THE CORONATION WAS the Royal Banquet. The very finest chefs on the Island of Albion were there to see that this superb celebration, perhaps the only one that they would ever witness in their lifetime, was everything that a magnificent historical event should be; the wild boar, venison, pheasant, and lamb had been smothered in steamed herbs and unhurriedly baked underground with hot rocks for days prior to the coronation. The dark interior of the castle was lit in a way that highlighted every royal, majestic, and grandiose aspect of this historic occasion. Keeping the torches lit properly and burning continuously without interruption was an art form and an acquired skill; only the proven were given this particular responsibility. The music consisted of a troupe that moved around the great hallway from cluster to cluster, which included a flute, a horn, a tambourine, a mandolin, and a small drum. The dance was by the numbers, and very rarely did one invent a new step and venture outside of the rigid tradition of the times.

And the guests were prattling on and on about their new king; some were saying that there were telltale signs in his youth that prophesied such success, so it did not come as a surprise to them – many of these prophets, however, were the very ones who, earlier, were calling him an eccentric and irresponsible carouser; but all agreed that it was rare to have a king that was trim, athletic, tall, slender, and handsome – yet there were a few that observed that his head was too big for his body, while others remarked that a large head with a strong chin was a not a flaw at all, but a desirable trait, and should be willfully bred into their population from this day forward.

To some the warrior-king concept was an oddity that many had difficulty in accepting, for kings were thought of as pampered, effeminate, dandies – as Edward had become in his later years. Harold Godwinson was a knight; he was a fighter -- with a scar here and a scar there; he was a man in his late thirties that could have easily passed for late twenties. Whatever the back and forth on the matter, all granted that his reign was to mark a new and very different era; for this reason it was a very exciting celebration for all.

Harold was doing his best to be polite, to smile and nod, and most of all, to make his guests and supporters feel as though they had been particularly successful that evening. He wanted to leave them with the impression that his victories were also their victories, and his defeats, their defeats. He felt that if he could accomplish these things with each guest than he would feel socially adequate – a feeling that was rare for him.

Edith-of-the-Swan's-Neck had worked her way through the crowd, and though they certainly had a history with each other, they both tacitly agreed not to parade that aspect – but she, however, did have a request:

"Dear Harold, it is my heartfelt honor to share in thy happiness and glory." And then dropping her voice with a quick glance behind her continued "And Harold, no more of that "Edith-of-the-Swan's-Neck nonsense! I want it mandated that such name-calling is prohibited from this day on. Will you see to that and make them stop?"

Harold smiled warmly. "I will try, Edith."

"Try? You're the king, Harold! Just tell them that there is a dungeon waiting for them. You're our king, and you must protect us." Edith smiled coyly. Harold nodded and returned the smile, and then turned to his brother Gyrth.

Gyrth was an honorable man, and a good soldier, though a tad headstrong in the field, according to some. He introduced his young lady friend to Harold; she had flaming red hair that accentuated her deep blue eyes and white gown. Gyrth said these words to his sibling,

"The destiny of Angle Land is in my brother's hands, and no finer captain did this ship ever have."

The two brothers hugged, and it was evident that there was a genuine fondness between them.

"And Gyrth, your participation in charting this course is essential. I need your help, Gyrth."

"You can count on it, brother," said Gyrth. He smiled and took a step back.

Tostig saw the opportunity to wish Harold well and stepped forward. There was no apparent jealousy in his manner. "Dearest brother, whatever differences we have had must now be laid aside for the infinitely larger purpose--and that is for the well-being of the citizens of the Isle of Albion. As Earl of Northumberland, with a heartfelt honor and respect, I hereby pledge my fealty to my King."

The two brothers hugged one another, and unbeknownst to Harold, this hug by Tostig had cued a soldier, masquerading as a steward to exchange a plate of Harold's food at the dining table while Harold was distracted.

"You have just lifted a heavy burden from my heart, Tostig," said Harold. "Please accept, from this day on, that my victories are your victories, and—"

But they were interrupted by a massive, yet infinitely playful two hundred pound Irish wolfhound that

Tostig had dognapped from a baron while in Dublin. Tostig's pet had pounced on a plate of pork and pranced victoriously away – a plate that was intended solely for the newly crowned Harold.

King Harold laughed at this, which sparked an uproar of laughter around the table. Tostig, however, didn't think this was at all amusing and motioned frantically to a cohort of Tostig's – the one who was masquerading as a steward. The steward comically began to chase the wolfhound throughout the banquet room, crossing the dance floor, zig-zagging around the sides, and successfully drawing the attention of the entire palace, who were in an uproar over the unexpected entertainment.

If it had been thought out and choreographed it could not have sparked more laughs. All watched as the steward would cagily sneak up on the wolfhound while it chomped the pork of the wild boar, but just as the steward leaped for him, the wolfhound would pick up the chunk of meat and playfully bound away, slipping and sliding across the polished stone floor, obviously delighted by this game.

But things took a nasty turn when the wolfhound dropped to its front knees and began to quake violently, followed by a horrible coughing as though it were choking. The massive dog frothed, wheezed, and then vomited. Within seconds the wolfhound had collapsed on the stone floor, where he lay very still.

There followed a silence of uncomprehending shock. The musicians had ceased playing, guests had stopped chattering, and those on the dance floor had become motionless; there was only the sound of a lone oblivious pigeon fluttering in the loft high overhead. After a moment someone shouted, "Treachery!" Another yelled, "Villainy!" This ignited a colossal uproar within the great torch lit hall as all that were sitting jumped to their feet. Gyrth, from the other end of the long dining table, yelled to Harold, "Where's Tostig?"

At that same moment two caped riders burst from the huge castle doors and galloped at full speed across the drawbridge and down the winding moonlit road, finally disappearing into the dark forest outside of London.

CHAPTER XVII

A Witch's Prophesy

ADELIZE SPENT MOST OF HER time staring out over the vast plains to the west, hoping to see a carrier pigeon homeward bound. How she would shower that pigeon with kisses! It would in her eyes be, not a pigeon at all, but a beautiful angel sent by the heavens above. Every second was a torment, every day a hell, and at times she despised waking up in the morning. There were more and more days where she wished that she would never wake up. She had lost considerable weight, and she wondered if Harold would be disappointed if he saw her so thin and gaunt.

She wasn't the only one that had these thoughts; her father would shake his head when he sighted her as she walked alone in the courtyard, and Matilda broke into sobs frequently. Matilda, who perhaps had been living vicariously through Adelize, had hoped that her beautiful daughter would find a happiness that had evaded her; so to watch the beautiful princess waste away was unbearably agonizing. It was not a happy time for William and his family.

Adelize, from the ledge of the balcony, looked straight down. There were several boulders at the bottom of the trellis. If she hit those boulders head first then the pain, the torturous longing, would leave and never come back. This was her thinking.

She sighed, and wondered if this were all part of the great scheme of life – the highs would never be high, unless there were lows -- she thought to herself. But how is one to endure these lows when they show up and refuse to budge, like parasitic guests that won't take a hint and leave? And then of course she would tell herself that she was a beautiful princess that had everything a person should ever want in this life, so she had no right – none whatsoever – to whimper over anything. These were her father's words, actually. They were meant to remind her that she was blessed, but she knew that her father was also tormented by Harold's defection, and once again she began to stare out over the horizon, hoping to see a white dot headed in her direction with the speed of an arrow. But perhaps the white dot had been intercepted by a hawk? Very possible! Maybe that was it!

Adelize no longer saw her thoughts as true thoughts; they were only an endless parade of grotesque jesters and clowns sent to torment her. Something had to change, and when she saw Squire Dudley in the distance round the corner with Spanish Dancer, she knew exactly what that change would be. A plan was hatched. She would speak with her father, and tell her that she was to send Harold a gift, while visiting the Island near the estuary.

That same day Princess Adelize spoke with her father. Her father liked the idea. He liked it a lot.

On a hilltop near the castle Harold was busy supervising the planting of the last of Adelize's flowers. There was a thin ground fog that was rapidly disappearing due to the morning rays of the sun. The hilltop was thick with saplings that had lost their leaves. He wondered out loud if this were the right time to be planting these flowers, but the keeper of the castle grounds assured Harold that it was alright, that the plants would fall asleep, and then wake up in the spring. Working with the grounds keeper, and now employed by the castle, was the crusty geezer. As it turned out he had a name after all; his name was Elroy, and Elroy happily assisted the grounds keeper in his duties around the castle grounds whenever possible. The old man turned out to be a first rate worker, but he was even better as a story teller.

Elroy, after glancing toward an old growth forest in the distance, speculated that certain dwarves were known to inhabit the underground of such ancient forests, and their abodes were accessible only by a secret knock on a tree, which was not a tree at all, but a secret passage to the underground. He intimated to Harold and the grounds keeper that he had actually visited a family of dwarves. They were very hospitable and the food was good, he said, but it was too difficult for him to get around, since the ceilings were so low, the hallways were narrow, and the beds were short – so he left, and as a departing gift he gave them a bow and arrow. But because of their diminutive size, they couldn't string the bow properly, so he took the bow and arrow back and he gave them his hat instead, which they were grateful for, and they said that it would make a nice chair for their infant, since their heads were too small to wear it. But, he said, he had nothing but good things to say about the dwarves, and if he could ever help them out in any way then he certainly would, and that no civilized man should ever bring harm to them.

Harold had a question: "What language did the dwarves speak?"

Elroy, looking the king straight in the eye, answered without hesitating that they spoke the same language that he did, which was "Keltic." He added that some on the mainland wrongly pronounced it as "Gaelic", but it was the same thing, he said. He added that the dwarves, like his people in Wales, had been on the island since the beginning of time, and before the invasion of the Northern Germanic tribe known as the Angles (Harold's people), the land all the way to the city of Rome was known as "Keltica".

Harold nodded respectfully as he listened to Elroy, for the old Kelt from the western shores had a way of telling these stories with such a calm and inner conviction that Harold could only nod his head and wonder... is this really true? If so, he concluded, then he would like to meet this family of dwarves, and descend into their domain for a visit; but this was a private thought that he had and was not shared with either Elroy or the grounds keeper, for there was always the chance that they were only having fun with the king. If they were, then he knew exactly what to do with them: Because of their bravery he would put them on the front lines in the next battle.

After a time the fog began to clear, and Harold could see the river Thames from where he was standing. What was he doing, he asked himself, as the newly crowned King of Angle Land, thinking about dwarves for god's sake? But he knew the answer: The reason was Adelize, and he would find himself turning his attention to anything and everything imaginable to escape the torment of a non-stop stream of images of his Adelize, which haunted him every second of every day.

He was in a predicament that (and he was resolute about this) no man in the history of the civilized world had ever been in. He was madly in love with the daughter of an extraordinarily powerful man who he greatly admired, and who he considered somewhat of a friend, yet fate had brutally intercepted this love he had for Adelize as a hawk intercepts a carrier pigeon

What now? Without question William, once his good friend, now considered him a traitor – so how could he see her, or even send her a message? What would he say to her, knowing that her father was railing against him at all hours of the day and night for having, in their eyes, betrayed them? William was not a passive man, so he knew that he would hear from him soon. But in the meantime how was he to communicate with Adelize?

Such were the thoughts of Harold as he watched a man who was still some distance away that was leading a horse in his direction. After a short while he could see that the man was one of his soldiers, and the horse he was leading was a giant. It was all black with one white sock on the right rear leg.

It was the Andalusian stallion – Spanish Dancer – and he snorted and shook his head when he saw Harold. Harold ran towards the approaching soldier, who handed him a note. Harold gently opened the note and immediately recognized Adelize's hand as he read the note aloud, rapidly the first time, and slowly the second:

"Where the Thames meets the sea,
That's where you'll find
lonely me. "

Shaking from head to toe, Harold proclaimed, "My god, she's here!"

All pain, grief, and inner torture was instantly lifted and magically replaced by a euphoria that only the person who is capable of loving another with the fullness of their entire being could ever know.

The soldier cupped his hands and held them for Harold. Harold put his foot in the cupped hands and vaulted onto the top of the huge Andalusian. Spanish Dancer ran sideways, arched his neck, laid back his ears, and bucked, throwing Harold high into the air; but fate was on Harold's side and he landed safely on the back of the stallion.

The warhorse charged forward with his neck arched, his nostrils dilated, and was nearly at full speed in three leaps. Spanish Dancer of Andalusia decided to give Harold the ride of his life. That was fine with Harold, but Harold wanted to make it clear to the warhorse that he and he alone would decide the destination. Off they went!

The soldier yelled from behind him that he should have an escort of knights, but Harold was long gone in a cloud of dust. He turned on a path towards the river and after a short burst through a wooded area he gave Spanish Dancer his head and felt the surge of the Pegasus, as the warhorse begin to churn, turning all heads, whether they were on land or on sea, for this was a sight that no human on earth could possibly ignore. But then what would they think if they knew that it was their Harold, their newly crowned king that was on the back of this beautiful creature that raced alongside of the river at a speed never seen before? Then what? He laughed so hard at the thought that he had to grab his wounded side for the rest of the journey.

Harold began to wonder if he was actually in control, or if he was simply a passenger, for the horse did not need to be guided; it seemed to know exactly where the estuary of the Thames was. Harold finally conceded that all he had to do was grip the mane tightly and he would be taken to Adelize by the fastest and most powerful horse that he had ever ridden in his life.

He raced through a small village, scattering geese and livestock, and then hit the open road next to flat fields. Harold laughed with joy as the Andalusian, whose hooves sounded to him like rolling thunder, swept past the dazzled on-lookers in the fields, who were pointing and shouting as he thundered past.

Because of the fog near the estuary of the Thames Harold was forced to slow the stallion down. He had turned onto the wet and shiny hard pack and was now in a slow lope. The only sound was that of the seagulls crying out and the channel waves crashing against the shore. He paused and looked in several directions before spotting the mast of a square rigger moored several hundred yards away, partially hidden by the fog. The sail, he could see, bore the Lion of Normandy with the right paw raised. He turned and galloped toward the boat when through the fog he saw a medium sized bonfire ahead. Directly behind the bonfire, sitting on a boulder and facing the ocean, was a solitary figure wearing a long black hooded robe. Harold, with an accelerating heart, brought his horse to a stop and dismounted. He took several steps toward the solitary figure and then called out to her.

"Adelize...!"

But she didn't stir. He tried again.

Adelize?"

This time the robed figure slowly turned toward Harold and stood up. She shed her robe and dropped it to the ground, and as the mist swirled around her Harold could see that this was not Adelize at all, but an octogenarian witch who began cackling and pointing at Harold while making punitive threats – the same threats that were made at William's exchange of sacred vows at the so-called farewell party before he left Normandy.

"A breach of the sacred vows causes the flesh to rot from the body while still alive, and Lucifer himself will hurl the offender into the lake of fire, and the devil Cherniborg will visit the offender, whereby the offender will thrash and roll in pain for all eternity in atonement for his breach, delighting the wiles of the black devil!"

The witch, now stark naked, spit in several directions while the flames from the driftwood fire crackled, hissed, danced and leaped. The witch, with long grey hair that hung to her knees, vomited in her hands and then tossed it across the bonfire at Harold. After smearing the remaining vomit on her dangling breasts and spitting in several directions, she leaped from the boulder with a cackle and ran naked into the fog, vanishing from Harold's sight.

Shocked, horrified, and confused Harold looked at the Norman sail once more. He took a few steps into the fog and was calling after her when out of the fog emerged William, the Duke of Normandy, holding his famous mace. The Duke of Normandy was combat ready. A second later two guards appeared behind William, also combat ready, bearing the shields of Normandy and attired in full fighting gear.

*"…..out of the fog emerged William,
the Duke of Normandy."*

All was quiet. Nothing could be heard except for the cry of a few sea gulls and the light crashing of the channel waves against the hard pack. Yes, William had liked Adelize's plan so much that he adopted it as his own. This was the way to meet Harold alone, without his military to protect him. It was brilliant! Of course Adelize was not happy that William had stolen her plan to meet Harold, but she would just have to stop her crying and accept that all Normans had to make their contributions to the cause of the greater Normandy – and this imaginative plan was her contribution -- for the destinies of the two most important nations in the world were now at stake. William took a battle-axe from one of his soldiers.

"They say that the axe is the favorite of the Anglish." William tossed the axe to Harold. As Harold caught the axe and stared back, he noticed that his heart was beating so loud that he wondered if William and his two soldiers could hear it.

It was then that William said these exact words, and once Harold heard them everything changed. "Prepare to defend yourself you treasonous, traitorous, lying, usurping coward."

Harold nodded. There was not a man alive that could say those words to him and continue to walk the earth. Harold was about to find out who William was, and William, it seems, was about to find out who Harold was.

"I need your guard's armor, his shield, and his broadsword." Harold tossed the battle-axe to the feet of William's soldiers. As Harold strapped on the breastplate, the greaves, and put on the hauberk he continued:

"As I said, William, I will follow the dictates of my conscience. I have been appointed King of Angle Land by Edward, and that law, in the Anglish tradition, supersedes all known law – including that of blood rights."

"Not so in Normandy!"

"We're in the land of the Angles now, not the land of the North Man!" Harold shot back. "But wherever we are, the one thing that people have never accused me of is a lack of honor."

Harold was nearly armored, and now he put on each gauntlet and then picked up his broadsword.

"You have challenged my honor today, and good sir, by doing that you have made a terrible mistake!"

It didn't take a keen eye to see that William was moved, but he fired back nevertheless:

"And Adelize? That is a vile and loathsome chapter in your life, Harold. To treat the purest soul that God has ever put on this earth as another one—"

At this point Harold erupted in a fury that none in Normandy had seen in him. "Then why didn't you bring her instead of that disgusting creature from hell – that goddamned witch? I would have joyfully married her -- today--right here -- with you William, performing the ceremony."

One of the soldiers standing next to William chuckled. Harold turned to him with a smile. "You like that?"

Big John smiled and nodded. "Yes, I did."

"You find it amusing?"

"Very!" he added, with a glance toward William, making sure that such brazen behavior was approved of by him before he continued along the same line.

"Then consider yourself the appetizer before the main course," said Harold. "Pick up your sword!"

"Take care, Harold. Big John is the trainer of my soldiers," advised William.

"Thank you for telling me, William! Now I won't feel so bad."

Big John looked toward William. After a moment William assented with a nod. Big John shrugged with a modest, restrained smile and picked up his broadsword. Big John pretended to warm up with a couple of impressive overhead slashes, whistling the air as he moved backward, forward, and then backward again, but suddenly in a surprise move Big John lunged toward Harold with a lateral swing. Harold ducked under this, and like a fighter rolling under a straight right and coming up with a left hook, countered with his own lateral swing catching Big John flush on the side of his unprotected neck and slicing clean through it as though it were a stalk of corn.

Big John's blood spouting head toppled from his body and hit the sand, while his torso teetered eerily before collapsing on the hard pack with a heavy thud.

Harold bent down and picked up Big John's helmet and gave it a vigorous shake. Big John's head fell out of the helmet and hit the sand. With his left hand he reached down and lifted up Big John's head by his hair and stood holding it nose to nose before asking this question:

"Where be your jibes now, Big John, trainer of soldiers? Are you still amused?" Big John's eyes were wide and his lips moved, as though he wanted to answer, but there were no lungs to drive the sound, so his thoughts on the matter shall forever remain a mystery.

Harold held the head of Big John straight out with his left arm, dropped it, and then with his right foot kicked Big John's head high into the air. The head spun round and round spewing a trail of blood and other matter before landing in the frothing estuary. A few seconds later it disappeared from sight and was never seen or heard from again.

Harold, still holding the helmet with his right hand, examined the craftsmanship and complimented William on the fine design of Big John's helmet before putting it on his own head. While fastening the strap underneath his chin he advised William that he was going to have to wait his turn, because there was somebody ahead of him, and then Harold pointed to the other soldier with his bloodied sword and said,

"You're next!" The color drained from the soldier's face, and he began glancing about at nothing in particular, when he suddenly sighted the mast of the square rigger. He turned to William and told him, with a theatrical urgency, that the square rigger was dragging anchor. William nodded and told him to take care of it. The soldier hastily moved out and disappeared into the fog.

After fastening the chin strap Harold observed William leaning down and picking up his mace. "Not the broadsword, brother William?"

"Not for you, Harold. It's the mace for you--the weapon that I know the best."

While making the final touches on his gear William said to Harold,

"Now I will ask you a final time, Harold. Will you step aside and allow me, William, Duke of Normandy, grand-nephew to Emma, and cousin to Edward the Confessor, to take my rightful place on the throne of Angle Land as its only blood heir?"

"Such a move would counter every oath I've taken in my life. I will not, William."

"Then prepare to die, Harold!"

William put on his helmet. Harold readied himself. The two men squared off. The fight began when William stepped forward with an overhead blow to Harold's shield, while Harold blocked and countered with a thrust, which William slipped, spun, and countered with another crushing blow that was blocked once again with Harold's shield.

Harold swung the broadsword low towards William's knees, but William had anticipated this and leaped straight up in the air; as the broadsword passed underneath him he watched as Harold exposed his left side. William knew what Harold's Achilles heel was; he knew the exact location of Harold's wound, and one clean blow with the mace on that wound would finish the fight.

William lowered his shield, hoping that Harold would throw a head-high lateral swing with his sword from the left that would expose Harold's left side, but Harold avoided the trap and grabbing his broadsword with both hands struck William's shield with such force that it nearly cleaved it in half. William took a step backward, hoping that Harold would try another one of his thrusts to close the distance. It worked! Harold thrust his broadsword toward William's mid-section. William turned and moved only the necessary three inches as the silver blade flashed past, and then countered to the crown of Harold's helmet with the mace, which knocked Harold back.

William observed that there was a sizeable dent in the helmet, and he began a series of powerful left and right blows with his mace to Harold's damaged helmet, catching him several times, but then Harold ducked, pivoted on his left foot, and suddenly Harold was no longer in front of William – he was behind him! William had never in his life seen this move. It was sheer devilry.

From behind William, Harold's sword came down on the top of William's helmet with a clang that could be heard all the way to Westminster Palace. William, stunned by the blow, wheeled about and took a defensive posture until he figured out where he was, which only took a second and a half -- but a second and a half can be a very long time in such a fight.

Harold went on the attack, marching forward with left and right lateral slashes. Angered by Harold's aggressiveness and surprise moves, William let out the ancient Norse war cry and ferociously countered, slamming the mace on Harold's left shoulder, and then on his right, all the while eyeing Harold's left side – and then in a lightning fast move William dropped down low and slammed Harold's sewed up jousting wound in a backhand with the butt of his mace.

Harold staggered backward. Two dozen green lights in the shape of worms swirled in front of Harold's face, and though the pain was far worse than any pain he had ever experienced in his life, he struggled to conceal it from his wily opponent. Harold went on the offence and continued with one slash after another, though he knew them to be somewhat wild, unfocused, and perhaps even desperate.

William again hammered Harold's helmet with the mace, and again Harold staggered back, seemingly dazed and disoriented, but as William was about to learn, this time it was only a ruse. William, sensing victory threw a hard lateral swing with the mace that Harold ducked under, pivoted, and came up behind William once again; and William once again cursed Harold's unusual devil moves, which he later described as "faster than a falcon's dive!" And again Harold sent a crushing overhead blow to the top of William's helmet – this time it separated several rivets.

William's helmet, now bent out of shape, was blocking his vision, so William stepped back and tore it from his head and threw it over his shoulder. Blood ran from William's crown, down his forehead, across his nose, and into his mouth. He ducked under Harold's slash and countered once again to the helmet of Harold. Harold was knocked back. Blood ran from his right eye. Harold tore his helmet from his head and tossed it to the ground to aid his vision. He was fighting with one eye now, and the wound from his left side had opened up and was showering the hard pack with blood.

Enshrouded in the dense fog were two young and valiant warrior-kings exchanging blow after blow, counter after counter, parry, thrust and slash, pivot, duck, slip and move. There came the clanging of iron, the crash of mace against shield, and the clash of the broadsword against shield and armor. Perhaps there were never two men in European history that had more indomitable wills, and had more at stake in the outcome of a single combat than these two former friends. The edge changed hands several times, but still there was no clear victor.

Finally William took a step back and held up his hand, signaling a short period of rest. He asked, "Do you agree?" Harold nodded and said, "I agree."

William leaned against the boulder that the witch had been sitting on. Harold leaned against the same boulder and placed his left hand over his wound to slow down the blood that was draining from his left side. Both struggled to catch their breath. William saw that Harold's eye was entirely swollen shut, bloody, and useless. Blood ran from his nose and his mouth. William had blood copiously running from the top of his head and over his entire face. William, through short gasps, finally spoke:

"Never has one individual surprised me in so many ways."

Harold spoke in short breaths as well, spraying blood on every syllable. "

"I wish I could say the same, William, but your legend preceded you, and you more than matched it." William nodded, and after a moment asked, "Are you ready, good sir?"

"I am," answered Harold.

Both, now helmetless, picked up their weapons and stood facing one another, ready for combat, but still breathing heavily. William could see that Harold's right eye was entirely swollen shut and if he swung the mace from that direction--with his left--Harold would never see it coming and his head would crack like an egg; but after a long moment of William looking at the valiant Harold spraying blood with every exhale, and flashing back to certain memories he had of him in Normandy, William lightly tossed his mace to the ground. Harold saw this and did the same with his broadsword. The two kings, finally overcome by pent-up emotions, stepped forward and hugged one another. It was an intense hug.

"Be a good king, my hard-headed brother!"

"I will do my best, William!"

Now clasping each other and looking directly in one another's eyes, William said "But here I come, Harold!"

Harold nodded. "I know, William."

William picked up his helmet and mace, turned away from Harold and walked into the fog. Harold staggered toward the boulder near the fire, leaned against it, but was afraid of sitting down because he felt that he would never rise again. A moment later Harold heard the snort of a horse and turned to see, emerging from the dense fog, Spanish Dancer slowly, very slowly, galloping past with the naked witch on his back. She screamed out as she passed Harold,

"September victory, October defeat,

Harold's reign, six luckless feet."

And then they vanished into the fog, or was Harold hallucinating? Moments later Spanish Dancer walked out of the fog, riderless this time, and stood next to the boulder. Harold, burning his final amount of energy, climbed onto the boulder and slid onto the back of Spanish Dancer. Spanish Dancer turned and slowly walked into the fog, carrying a bloody and severely wounded newly crowned King of Angle Land on his back.

CHAPTER XVIII

The Prophesy of Starlings

WITHIN THE CASTLE GROUNDS WILLIAM stood with several blacksmiths, who were dressed with heavy leather gloves that reached to their elbows. Each had thick leather around their neck and torsos, and all were heavy set, with broad shoulders and thick arms. Standing slightly apart from William were several mounted knights. To the rear, through the doorway, were huge blast furnaces that would explode with a white hot light, and then in an instant return to an intense burning red. William was trying to talk over the clanging of hammer and anvil when one of the blacksmiths stepped through the doorway and told his army of craftsman to hold the work; it became quiet and William resumed.

He was holding a helmet and turning it over and over; it was the same helmet that he had used when he had fought Harold, and it was, according to William, a fine example of the structural defects of their current line. As William spoke the blacksmiths leaned in and savored every single word, nodding as though they understood, even if that wasn't always the case.

"If we stay with the arch, then we have a rigid helmet, but you can see right here where we strayed from the design and this is why you have the defects here, and also right here."

William glanced at several of his knights and yelled for Tremaine, the handsome smoothie whom William had seen exchange flirtatious glances with Matilda at the Brittany joust. Tremaine slid from his destrier and with haste reported to William.

"Tremaine, we need for you to try this helmet on, so the smiths can see how it fits."

Tremaine tried on the helmet and then looked inquiringly at William and his blacksmiths. After a moment he took a few steps, turned gracefully, and then in a modified strut took another several steps in the opposite direction, turned, and then froze in position while rotating his head in various directions, giving William a profile to the left, and a profile to the right, and all the while displaying his near perfect teeth with a wide smile.

From there Tremaine began turning is body from side to side, and seconds later he was preening, wagging his shoulders and showing them this angle and that, and while doing this he continued to maintain his happy smile.

"How does it fit?" asked William.

Tremaine became very serious when he replied, "A little on the loose side, Duke William."

William bashed Tremaine across the helmet with his mace. The crack was so loud that several of the knight's horses reared and took steps on their hind legs. Tremaine collapsed and hit the ground with a moan. William bent over and removed the helmet from Tremaine's head and showed it to the blacksmiths, who eagerly leaned forward to get a closer look at William's fine example.

"This is what I'm talking about. This amount of indentation should have never occurred for that slight of a blow. We need both lateral and vertical reinforcement—utilizing both the Roman arch and the Prussian method of riveting."

William handed the helmet to the chief blacksmith, who accepted it while nodding his understanding.

"How many, Sire, do you need?" asked the blacksmith. William, while mounting his horse replied that he would need several thousand before the equinox, further adding that he was to triple his work force while the artisans built more furnaces. The blacksmiths came near collapsing next to Tremaine when they heard the size of the order and the time frame. They steadied one another while remaining fixed on William.

"Any questions?" asked William.

In unison they shook their head no. William bid them farewell and left. He was followed by his knights and one riderless horse.

The day was cloudless and windy. The trees were bare. Harold and Bishop Verser were seated near the balcony window of Harold's sleeping quarters in the castle and were staring out over the vast city of eighteen thousand inhabitants known as London. In the distance a huge flock of starlings were changing forms with a fluidity that was mesmerizing. The flock, which seemed to number approximately the same as the inhabitants of London, was swirling, twisting, diving, looping, spiraling, elongating, and then suddenly compressing – all in unison! Both Harold and the bishop were fascinated, but found that they were dogged by the same question: "How do they do it? How do the members on the west side of the flock turn in unison at exactly the same second as the members on the east side of the flock – and the north side, and the south side? The massive flock of starlings seemed to be controlled by a central authority that was able to communicate direction to thousands at exactly the same millisecond. Did they have a queen, like a hive of bees? Even if it was established that the starlings did have a central authority, it still didn't answer how the command was given by that queen and then received at exactly the same split second by the thousands so that the directional change happened at a precise degree in perfect harmony without massive collisions and chaos.

The bishop observed that if all the sages, sorcerers, and druids on the island were put in a single room, not a one, or all of them together, could figure out this phenomenon of nature. Harold agreed with the bishop.

Harold said to the bishop that he, in fact, greatly envied the starlings; for if he as king could engender that kind of communication and harmony with the thousands of soldiers under his command then his military would be the finest in the known world. Both he and the bishop were doing their best to understand the nature of this mystery, but they didn't get very far.

For the bishop, who once traveled east down the Dnieper River as a Varangian, the fluid clouds of starlings always prophesied the outcome of looming battles; and their sages took these prophesies seriously. The bishop felt that there was a clear and unequivocal prophesy in their united mass movements today, but seemed reluctant to share that ominous prophesy with Harold. The one aspect that they both agreed on was that it was an extraordinarily beautiful sight -- right up there with lightning storms.

But finally Harold had to turn his head away from the window and shield the light with his hands. Bishop Verser asked if it was still too bright for his eyes to look outside, and Harold nodded that it was. Harold, with some effort stood up, holding onto a bedpost, and took a few steps.

"Well, that's an improvement!" said the bishop, trying to smile. Harold sat back down and ran his hand across several lumps on his face. His right eye was black and swollen, but the swelling had decreased some, revealing a blood-red eye hiding underneath. The bishop leaned in and observed Harold's left eye, and noted that the pupil was twice its normal size. He told Harold that such expansion was usually accompanied by a severe blow to the head. The bishop frowned and shook his head; he couldn't hold back any longer:

"You were lucky you weren't killed," said the bishop. "It happens all the time when people are thrown from their horses." After a moment he continued with some force, "That horse is dangerous! You shouldn't ride it unaccompanied...in fact, you shouldn't ride it at all! We've had it isolated from the other horses because it nearly killed a couple of our finest stock. Just look at yourself! You can barely walk. You can't continue like this, Harold. You are no longer a young boy running wild. You are king now. You just can't jump up and race through the forest and down the roads on a crazy horse whenever you feel like it. You can't gallivant all over the countryside jousting nameless at these tournaments and willfully put yourself in the path of danger anymore. It's all different now! You are now responsible for something a thousand times higher than yourself!"

Harold felt as though he were being hammered by William all over again. All had assumed that he had been thrown from his horse, "While traveling as fast as any arrow", according to witnesses. He allowed them to believe that because he had no strength to tell them otherwise. He didn't have the strength now, and so he raised his hand and said in a gentle manner,

"Bishop…enough! It wasn't the horse. The horse had nothing to do with it. It was something else…and that is all I'm going to tell you today. I don't have the strength to tell you otherwise. In a few days maybe I will tell you everything. I'm going back to sleep. In the meantime see that Spanish Dancer remains isolated and is well taken care of. He is my horse, and by god I will ride him again. And Bishop, we need to summon the witnamagote! Next week we'll have to have a meeting in the great hall. It's urgent!"

The bishop nodded and asked Harold if he could fetch him anything; Harold whispered that a cup of water would be very nice, and then he fell into a deep sleep before the bishop could move from his chair.

CHAPTER XIX

Tostig and William

TOSTIG HAD BEEN APPEALING TO William's well-known and boundless quest for power for some time in the great castle hallway in Normandy. William sat elevated next to Matilda, and both were listening with great reserve to the brother of Harold Godwinson, the new king of the Angles.

William saw that Tostig, when asked a direct question, had a tendency to crab sideways and shrug his shoulders while answering. To both William and Matilda, this was an unsavory trait that did not go unnoticed by either.

With his customary anxiety-ridden whine, Tostig was at times calm and exact, which would be followed by flattery, and then humor, and then he would abruptly shift to anger and outrage. He was certain that things at this point were going even better than he had hoped, and this encouraged him to be unusually open with his two new friends, and from time to time he even felt bold enough to venture across the line of a rigid décor into an area of being cozy with one another, even though neither William nor Matilda had encouraged him in the slightest to do so.

"North Umbria's allegiance is to me – not Harold! North Umbria shares my outrage! I've never wanted to rule over any other territory except my home, North Umbria. That's all! And now the demented dotard, the late Edward, whose faculties were in absentia at the moment of his death, now played directly into the wily usurper's hands--the hands of my notoriously carousing wenchifying brother, Harold, the fox."

He waited for the desired response, and seeing nothing, decided to delve into an area that William could no longer feel casual about.

"And of course he never stopped debasing you--and your elegant wife--at every opportunity."

"What did he say about me?" asked William.

"He told me that he personally beat you in jousting--he said that you were a coward, and that you were a man that could not be trusted---on and on he went, ad infinitum. It was boring, and after a while I stopped listening to his meaningless rant. I knew it was all false -- but that's my brother Harold, which I played no part in choosing! I've known him for a long time."

There was a lengthy pause as Tostig waited once again for William to respond, but it soon became evident that William was not going to respond as hoped, and so Tostig continued, now rolling out his heavy weapons,

"And forgive me, I hesitate to even mention this, but he also said that your wife was unattractive, but as I stand before her now, I am stunned at how a human being can twist the truth for his own ends. Matilda, if I may say, is one of the loveliest women I have ever seen; and you, honorable sir, I would trust with my life."

"Let's come to the point! What is it you want, exactly?" asked William.

Tostig was slightly shaken by William's brusque reply, but continued on.

"An alliance, to crush Harold the usurper! To come to the point, as you say, we should form a pincer movement--I'll lead the forces of North Umbria from the north into London, while you attack from the southern shore. Harold, the usurping fox will suddenly squeal like a wild pig writhing on the end of a spear as his false empire is caught in this pincer movement and crushed like an egg under the wheel of truth and honor."

William suddenly seemed interested in the words of Tostig. He turned to Matilda.

"Matilda, my dear, there is a certain breed of people, like Tostig, for example, who are..."

William paused, and then turned to Tostig with a warm smile. Tostig smiled warmly in return, and then William continued,

"…who are neither creative nor productive, but survive by calumny only! These calumniators, who blacken the reputation of the honorable, are hell's most pernicious."

Tostig's smile vanished. William stood from his chair and took several steps down to the floor, slowly walking toward Tostig. Tostig took a few steps backwards, nervously glancing at his two guards that had entered the hallway with him.

William continued walking toward Tostig, saying "Harold said none of these things. Harold is an honorable man!"

One of Tostig's guards, taking a cue from him, immediately stepped between William and Tostig, but just as the cobra paralyzes the chicken with his stare, so did William paralyze this guard with a single glance. Perhaps it was because of the enormous celebrity of William, but the guard became inoperable; his body refused to obey his mind, and his teeth began to chatter. William gently pushed him aside and told Tostig to take a seat, which Tostig did immediately without knowing why.

William asked him if he would like a glass of mead. Tostig nodded, and a servant ran for two cups and a tankard of mead. William sat across from Tostig and continued to talk in a manner that suggested that everything was completely normal; he first asked Tostig if he would be offended if he did not join him in drinking the mead, because of his violent stomach. Tostig assured William that he would not be offended in the least, but then wondered if he were about to be poisoned by William. William continued in a gentle manner, speaking in a way that suggested that Tostig had come to him as a friend in need, and he was only there to help him through this challenging time.

"The man that you want to see, Tostig, is Haarald Hardrada. He shares your outrage. He, like you, sees himself as the man that should be ruling Angle Land.

Tostig glanced over at Matilda, who was still sitting in her throne. She had remained motionless throughout. He smiled and nodded to her, but there was no response.

"Did you hear what I said?" asked William.

The servant hastily sat an empty cup in front of Tostig and then poured Tostig the fermented honey known as mead.

"Well yes," answered Tostig, "but my question is, don't you see yourself as being in contention for the crown also?" This question was followed by an innocent shrug from Tostig, who had brought the mead to his lips, but pretended to be so enthralled by William's answer to this question that he slowly sat the mead back down again without taking a sip, hoping that this would not be noticed William.

"It's absolutely true that I, like you, don't think that your brother Harold has a legitimate claim for the Anglish crown – but Normandy, for the time, is challenging enough for me; but this conversation is not about me, Tostig, it's about you! If you were to join forces with Haarald Hardrada, who wishes to invade the north, he could easily take York by himself, and then the both of you could sweep down into London through your corridor, North Umbria, recruiting in your land as you move south, and from there into London. Keep in mind, Tostig, that Hardrada has never lost a battle in his life. This is your man, and I am sure that he would be open to the idea of joining forces with you."

To Tostig, everything that William was saying made perfect sense, except for one minor detail. "But what happens after Hardrada and I defeat my brother Harold? What then, since both Hardrada and I feel entitled to the crown?

"I can't figure everything out for you, Tostig, but it's getting late, and you should be on your way before darkness reigns." William stood. Tostig stood also, and held out his hand in gratitude, but without taking his hand or saying anything further William turned and walked to Matilda. She extended her hand, which he took, and after she stood they both turned into the hallway and walked up the stairs without parting words of any kind. Tostig was left standing alone with his hand sticking out, despising William's rudeness and lack of respect, but intrigued by his strategy of combining forces with the undefeated Viking of the north, Haarald Hardrada.

Sometime later Tostig, still smarting from William and Matilda's open show of disrespect, stood shaking his fist at William and screaming at the top of his lungs while the sails bulged with a strong wind. He was far from shore by now, and William was nowhere in sight, but Tostig still saw to it that William would not get away with such a crass display of insolence toward him.

"You're a filthy bastard! Your mother was the whore of Falaise and you're a filthy bastard!"

Tostig turned to the captain and shouted over the intense wind and the flapping of the sails, "Too much inbreeding, Captain. William's parents were brother and sister, you know."

"I thought you said he was a bastard?"

"That too! The brother and sister were never married -- you fool!" After a moment Tostig continued, "And mind your compass, Captain! It's your job to get us to Flanders, not to school me about your goddamn philosophy -- which has obviously failed! Understand Captain? No more ridiculous questions!"

CHAPTER XX

Two Very Different Meetings

DAYS LATER THERE WAS A meeting of the Council of the Wise, better known as the Witenagemote. This council of the island's most influential found themselves in the midst of a volatile debate. Eadwulf of Mercia stood and shouted to the others while waving his sword,

"Let the Normans invade! We'll cut them down as they get out of their dragon boats!"

A resounding cheer went up through the King's Hall. The elderly warrior, Wulfgeat, stood; the room suddenly quieted, and all waited to hear the words of the seasoned fighter.

"I, Wulfgeat of Anglia, have fought with Hardicanute of the Danes, Godric of Iceland, and William's very own father—'Robert the Devil' of Normandy. I will say in order to launch a full scale invasion of this island more ships would be necessary to carry more soldiers than there are in all of the north countries combined. This I know: No invader, including the son of 'Robert the Devil', has this many ships. Fear not such an invasion from the Normans!"

Wulfgeat sat down and there were more cheers throughout the King's Hall as Harold stood and begun to speak.

"If we were dealing with ordinary times, ordinary people, and ordinary nations, I could begin to understand some of the arguments presented here today -- but we are not! We are dealing with what will someday be recognized as one of history's most extraordinary figures --William the Conqueror. He has been fighting in the field since age nineteen, and he has never lost a battle. If we ignore the Normandy threat, then peace and victory will ignore us, brothers – and we will lose this land – which is held as ours by the sword only – not by a piece of paper, and certainly not by hopes and prayers!"

All in the great hall applauded their new leader's words. Edward was right; Harold was the man to unite the Angles into a battle-ready force; but not now. Not just yet. It was too early, said the men of parliament, as they conferred amongst each other. Even discussing this with one another was a nuisance, because it just took more time away from sitting in their manors in front of a massive fireplace, tended to by their beautiful women who would hand them a mug of spicy ale while their feet were being massaged by specialists imported from a faraway eastern country whose name they could never pronounce. Yes, Edward the Confessor was right: The Angles had been enjoying the protection of the forty kilometer moat known as the "Anglish Channel" for so long that many of their citizens had become lazy and indifferent. But on the other side of the channel things were very different.

———◆———

Within William's large castle there was a meeting of the Commune Concilium. The tone of the meeting was infinitely different in every way than that of the Witenagemote. William was the speaker, the only speaker, and there was no opposition – only a loud and boisterous assent.

"You who have borne witness to the blood oath of Harold of the Anglish, and you who have borne witness to the violation and treachery of that oath, the sacrilege, the disrespect, the betrayal---"

There was a loud murmur in the room.

"What say you now, brothers? Do we invade? Do we take our rightful place in history as the blood heirs to the throne of the Angles? Do we take Angle Land?"

The Commune Concilium, in a single thunderous response, roared their approval in favor of the invasion. And now combining the Old Norse mythology with their new and transitional belief in Christianity, William proceeded to lash them into a frenzy.

"Then we shall loose upon the island of the Angles a furious storm of lightning and thunder such as the world has never seen!"

The Normans jumped to their feet and shouted their approval.

"This will be the battle that our savior sends the God of our fathers, Odin, armed with the sword of triumph to appear on the battlefield and guide his sons to victory!"

There was more thunderous stomping and applause as the sons of the Norseman yelled and screamed in ecstasy.

"And may our savior send the blessed angels, the Valkyries, to rescue the fallen heroes and guide them to the home of our Viking fathers, Valhalla, the great warrior castle in the sky!"

There was more thunderous applause, stomping, screaming, and yelling from inside the castle.

"And may our warrior fathers, from Valhalla look down upon this conquest of the Anglish by their Norseman sons and know that the torch had been passed, not to sniveling cowards who shrink from the duty of their fathers, but to those who understand courage, who understand conquest, who understand sacrifice, and to those who understand the love of battle!"

The Commune Concilium became a howling frenzied mob who danced on the tables and in the aisles yelling, "Invasion! Invasion! Invasion! Onward to Angle Land! May God be with us!"

CHAPTER XXI

The Holiness of a South Wind

ON THE COAST OF NORMANDY, William stood looking at the colossal fleet of ships that he had acquired through his own massive shipbuilding effort combined with the generous donations from many of the countries of mainland Europe, which had not seen a fleet of eight hundred ships since Julius Caesar, over a thousand years earlier.

A simple glance at the numerous flags that were flying above the ships revealed another problem – no south wind to launch the invasion. The absence of a south wind was not only unusual; it was unheard of at this time of year.

This unforeseen curse created several problems: For one, his soldiers were stranded on the Normandy beach with their attack anxiety at combat level. Most of these soldiers were young, aggressive, hot heads that lived for confrontation. If you put them on a beach for several weeks with nothing to do then it's only a matter of time before they begin fighting one another out of tedium and monotony. He had instructed the cadre to invent athletic games and challenges to whittle away the time so that they wouldn't maim and kill each other out of boredom, but this strategy only worked for a while, and then they were back to starting fights with each other. Something had to be done.

But the lack of a south wind gave birth to an even larger problem – the question as to whose side God was on began to elbow its way into the equation. Surely if God sanctioned the invasion then there would be a south wind; there was not a soul in the world, regardless of their sympathies, that could ignore that simple premise. This left more than a few scratching their heads and thinking, "Maybe he talked too much about Odin, Thor, and those Valkyries in his rallying speeches....instead of Jesus, who he never really mentioned... come to think of it."

The immediate problem that had to be solved, as William saw it, was to answer this nagging question once and for all without further delay. To him the solution was clear; he had to receive the blessing of the Pope. That would do it, for if the invasion were sanctioned by God, then those who opposed it in any way would then be seen as blasphemous devils that deserved to be skewered.

The other advantage was that it was well known that if a soldier died in a battle that had been blessed by the Pope, then he was guaranteed "eternal salvation". This single item removed the fear of being killed in battle for many of the soldiers who truly believed in god and the afterlife; for who wouldn't exchange their miserable existence on earth for a place in heaven, where everything was whatever a person imagined perfection to be?

William promptly dispatched an envoy to Rome to meet with the Pope and secure the Pope's blessing so that during the invasion he could fly the flag of the Papal Bull -- hence all could see for themselves that his invasion was sanctioned by God.

He was successful. The Pope had acknowledged that William had been generous in his building of cathedrals in Normandy, generous in his donations to the Vatican, and had for the most part treated members of the clergy with respect. In his personal life he was known to be faithful to his wife, Matilda, and not an incorrigible womanizer like his father, Robert the Devil. All in all he was the perfect candidate for the Pope's blessing.

Once it was known that the Normans were flying the flag of the Papal Bull, then those who were ambivalent about fighting for the Normans signed up for the invasion; they were now doing God's work instead of just plain soldiering.

As if that weren't enough, William then proclaimed that those soldiers who fought for Normandy and conquered the Anglish were entitled to the spoils of war. Simply stated, it would be mandated that many of the Anglish would either be killed or driven from their lands, their cities, their towns, their farms, and their houses; a shortage of Anglish males would be intentionally created as part of the plan. Even their women would be confiscated and distributed to the Norman soldiers who had validated themselves by fighting to the end and entering London. For young men that had nothing, the promise of a new and prosperous life with an obedient wife was very persuasive to them.

That promise, however, led to a fiery opposition by some, including his brother Odo and several members of the clergy. It was considered a bad strategy, for there would be rebellions and uprisings by the Anglo Saxon that could go on for centuries following the invasion. The clergy and many others used the strategy of Caesar as a paradigm:

Caesar was almost always surprisingly generous to those he conquered, they argued. He set out to convince the vanquished that their lives would actually be much better as a result of the invasion, and he was usually successful in making that promise happen. The clergy pointed out that the Romans ruled the Keltic lands (Keltica) from the river Po, west of the Rhine, all the way to Belgium and the south of Britain by utilizing

that simple strategy. Yes, there was an occasional upris-
ing by the likes of a Vercingetorix or a Boudicca -- but
ultimately those uprisings were quelled. For the most
part that strategy worked perfectly for five hundred
years and only came to an end when the Romans left
voluntarily because Rome was imploding.

William listened to these arguments by the clergy
and others; he understood what they were saying; but
he liked the idea of the Normans becoming the abso-
lute owners of the Anglish island – because then the
conquest was *irreversible*! Yes, there would always be uprisings by the Angles, the Saxons, and the Danes; so
the Normans would just have to build castles to control
and eliminate the loose confederations of outlaws who
would be prowling the forests. William argued that,
"The Anglo-Saxons can sit in their forests and sing all
the songs they want around their tiny campfires about
their 'robbing hoodlums', but one spear through the
chest of their outlaw Robin Hoods and those songs
would quickly fade away."

Duke William, they could see, was not an easy man
to argue with.

CHAPTER XXII

Tostig and Hardrada

In a late afternoon on the Norwegian coastline near a village on the North Sea, Haarald Hardrada, King of Norway, conferred with his brother, Lothgar. Both men were seated outdoors and facing the sea, whose rolling whitecaps seemed to be warning all mariners, "Not today!" as the huge waves crashed with an anger seldom seen on the southern shore.

Out of earshot sat Tostig with a several mariners. Tostig was nervously awaiting a decision. While biding his time he watched as a lone sea gull struggled to fly upwind. After a while the gull finally resigned, dropped down to the beach and faced north to wait it out. Tostig stared at the bird, thinking that he would like to do exactly the same thing, which was to lay on the beach, face north, and go to sleep until all this nonsense went away, and then when he woke up things in his life might be rosy again.

Hardrada, another genuine warrior-king, immediately made his feelings known to Tostig that he had a claim to the throne of Angle Land. Tostig could see that Hardrada's claim was entirely delusional. It was based on the idea that his co-ruler in earlier times, Mangus, was related to a Dane that had claims to the throne. Once Mangus passed away Harold Hardrada thought that the tenuous claim of his co-ruler should be passed on to him as a matter of inheritance, and that he should become king of the land of the Angles.

Because nobody dared argue with this massive hulk, who carried an axe with him wherever he went, over time this gooey oyster of a claim crystallized into a black pearl within Hardrada's huge clam-like skull.

While Hardrada and Lothgar conferred at a distance, it was clear that neither had a good impression of this Tostig fellow. They, like William, had observed that Tostig had a tendency to crab sideways while shrugging his shoulders when asked a direct question. Lothgar further felt that it was clear that Tostig was the type of leader that was almost always putting his own interests ahead of his people.

"I agree with you, Lothgar," said Hardrada, "and I would just as soon run a leather thong through one of his ears and out the other--and then hang his head on my belt. But for the present, his head attached to his body serves me better."

"Why?" asked Lothgar.

"He knows the geography of the north, besides, if all able-bodied males are on the Angle's south shore defending against the Norman invasion, as Tostig says, then York would be that much easier. We could secure a foothold there, and then when the time is right turn south, go through Tostig's North Umbria, recruiting from his domain as we move south, until finally we are in London." Once we get to London, we'll figure out what to do with Tostig.

Lothgar nodded in agreement. They both looked over at Tostig. Tostig took this as a sign that they had reached some kind of understanding so he stood and approached them with a smile.

CHAPTER XXIII

The Invasion of York

IT WAS EARLY MORNING. THE direct sunlight had not yet traveled to the north of Angle Land, and the colors of the early light were blue, gray, and green. A large fleet of square-rigged Viking warships approached the estuary of the Humber River from the North Sea. The massive Hardrada was amusing his fellow soldiers in the flagship by tormenting Tostig. It didn't take long for Hardrada to conclude that Tostig was the perfect punchline for all of his jokes, and the travel time would go by much faster for his warriors if he talked openly about the dreams that he had.

"And I also dreamed of a fearful demoness who rode howling on the back of Fenris the wolf. The demoness would feed the bloody carcasses of the Anglish to Fenris, whose appetite for the squealing Anglish was insatiable." Hardrada turned to Tostig, whose head was barely peeking out of the skin of a reindeer and asked, "What could this mean? Is it a sign, Anglish Man?"

The Vikings, scantily clad, laughed at Tostig's discomfort. Lothgar, from the bow of the square rigger turned and asked, "How do you know this is the Humber River?"

Hardrada and Tostig leave Norway for York

"I grew up here," said Tostig, while shivering beneath reindeer skins.

Once they were out of the North Sea they in unison picked up their oars and quietly dipped them in the water; the huge Viking fleet headed up the Humber moving against a mild September current. Before long they were headed up the River Ouse.

A young boy who was tending goats on a hillside turned to see the largest fleet of boats that he had ever seen in his short life emerge like silent ghosts from the early morning mist -- and they were on his river, headed toward his village. Soon after, the two hundred and fifty Viking warships that carried the trained warriors had hit the town of York hard and fast –and this while most people were still sleeping in their beds. There was a brief battle, but one glance at the eight thousand battle-ready Vikings compelled most of the townspeople to throw down their weapons, hoping that immediate surrender and cooperation would save their families.

The young boy's inner torment of not being able to warn his friends and families was overwhelming, but he had also realized that his greatest use was to find help as soon as possible, so he set out on the most rigorous and demanding journey that he had ever taken -- to find a known monastery.

Hours later the young boy entered a monastery near the River Ouse. The monks gathered and listened with heavy hearts to the young boy's tale; the monks knew all about the Vikings and their surprise raids. It was less than an hour after the boy's appearance that a rider burst from the monastery and rode toward the noon September sun – straight south to London. Several carrier pigeons were released carrying notes to the same town in case the rider should become ensnared in a tragedy of some kind—and then later in the darkness two more pigeons were released in case those released in the day should be hit by raptors.

———◆———

Haarald Hardrada had ruled Norway for twenty years. He wrote poetry, played the harp, was interested in Christianity, but invoked the Nordic gods in time of war. He was a massive, well-built athletic Viking who was known to have fought entire battles on the front lines, swinging an axe or a sword with both hands. He had a history of conquest in Western Europe or deep into Russian territories – but in the end it was always conquest. As an experienced conqueror, like Caesar, he stressed to the vanquished that their lives were to be improved from this day on; from his experience this minimized uprisings and encouraged cooperation.

Within days he was sitting in the center of York on a makeshift throne. There were several thousand Vikings in attendance, which nearly exceeded the population of York itself. After a while he stood and turned in different directions while facing the crowd, and out of his massive chest thundered a surprising sincerity and calm as he said these words:

"On this September day in 1066, is one of the most blessed of my life. We are here as your liberators, not your oppressors. Our goal is to establish a trade route between Norway and the north of Angle Land that someday will expand to the length and breadth of this beautiful island. All will prosper, all will benefit, and that is my goal. I pledge, as your King of the North, to rule with wisdom and justice, and may Odin be with you all. Now if you'll excuse us, my men and I have work to do. We are building a fortification at Stamford Shire Bridge."

Hardrada stepped down and with a long walking staff headed for Stamford Shire Bridge followed by his Vikings. As he left, Tostig watched in utter amazement as many of the townspeople roared, "Liberators...liberators...liberators, " and others standing next to Tostig were yelling out, "Long live Hardrada, our king," even after Hardrada had disappeared from sight. Yes, the old Viking knew how to attack, subdue, and turn the entire population of a town into his willing servants, all within a matter of days.

CHAPTER XXIV

King Harold II Marches to York

IN LONDON KING HAROLD WAS standing next to a lathered horse. The exhausted rider was listening as Harold read a message while his brother Gyrth looked over his shoulder. There were other cadre officials standing nearby, craning their necks. After a moment Harold looked up at the others, and quietly said, "It's Haardrada of Norway. The old Viking just can't sit still. He has taken York, and now it's only a matter of time before he moves south, planting the Norwegian flag acre by acre until he reaches London."

Gyrth suggested splitting the troops; he would march to York with some of the men, while his brother Harold would stay with the rest of the troops and continue to monitor the south shore. But Harold felt that the risk of a Norman invasion after the equinox was greatly reduced because of the wind direction and the known violence of the seas. His generals agreed that an invasion had never happened after the equinox.

King Harold also argued that the invasion in York was real, while the invasion from Normandy remained speculative because of the fickle winds, so it must be concluded that the threat of the Vikings in the north had to be eliminated once and for all. If the Hardrada invasion was not checked, then the Norwegians would pour into the north of Angle Land and sweep down through Tostig's North Umbria – and that part of the island would be forever lost to Norway.

There was much back and forth regarding this issue, but ultimately it was decided that the entire military should leave London and began an impossibly long and arduous two hundred mile march to Yorkshire, where they would, at the end of this journey, fight eight thousand Vikings led by an undefeated warrior-king known as Haarald Hardrada – but first they had to convince the witnamagote.

Once this had been reported to the town the London the bells rang with a ferocity that had never been heard before by the citizens of the island's largest town. It was alarming; many of its citizens were running as fast as they could without always knowing where they were headed.

Inside the great hall, built with huge wooden beams, colossal grey stones, and lit by massive torches -- there was another meeting of the witenagemote.

This time the tone of the meeting was entirely different than the previous, and several of the members were no longer thinking of having their feet massaged in front of a fireplace while drinking hot ale – they were now wondering whether they should flee or fight – but those were few in number. On this day it was the voice of the fighter that prevailed; Harold stepped onto a chair, and from the chair he stepped onto the surface of the table of the witenagemote so that those in the farthest corners of the great hallway could hear and see as well as those who were seated close, for today the hallway overflowed with, not just the decision-makers, but the fighters from the streets, the hills, the coasts, the sea, and the countryside.

There were hundreds more who stood outside, many wearing their warrior tunics with battle-axe in hand. Harold Godwinson, now Harold Rex the king, quieted the huge hallway by barely raising his hand. There was a lengthy silence before the new king began -- a king that all could see had scars and scrapes here and there; it was a youthful well-muscled warrior-king that was about to speak to them, and thankfully, not a bed-ridden fop.

"When the leaf turns yellow and falls from the tree," began King Harold, "then it is answering the iron rule of nature. But our leaf is green; our country is in its youth, and it is not about to fall from the tree, *nor will it be torn from the branches by the enemy* – and that is, my brothers, OUR IRON RULE! It is the iron rule of the Germanic tribes – the Angles, the Saxons, and the Danes! We will remind the world once again that no one, including the Romans, has ever conquered the tribes of Germania -- and the Vikings of Norway are about to learn exactly why that is!"

The sons of Germania jumped to their feet and heartily applauded their new leader.

"Our fathers before us fought with a courage and valor that will be sung throughout the ages, but if our fathers had hesitated, then we would not be standing here today on this beautiful island as free men; we would be in chains; we would be in Roman cages, we would be tethered like trained dogs; and we would, every one of us, be the subject of our inferiors had it not been for the loyalty, the courage, and the sacrifice of those that have gone before us."

There was more thunderous stomping and applause as those within the great hall yelled and screamed their support.

"And today all that has been fought and died for in our glorious history is now laid at our doorstep to defend. But I don't need to speak to you today of these matters. I can see that your hearts have already whispered these things to your minds, for most here today have taken the shields, the helmets, and the swords of their fathers from their walls above their mantles and brought them here today -- so I don't think I need to ask, 'What say you now, my brothers?', because you have told me what your answer is – and that answer is,

"ON TO YORK! DEATH TO THE NORSEMEN!"

The massive king's hallway thundered with approval, while Harold shouted over the continuous applauding, shouting, and the pounding of shield against sword.

"Our day has come brothers. Today the torch has been passed to the sons of this great land, and today is the day that the eagle of Albion flies, for we will answer that call in the glorious tradition of our fathers and drive what is left of Hardrada's invaders from our shores and into the sea."

In the streets of London the Anglish soldiers were lined in columns of ten as far as the eye could see. Harold Godwinson, mounted on Spanish Dancer, waved his sword and said these final words to his men:

"ON TO YORK, ONE AND ALL, MY BROTHERS!"

The island's people as a whole, united for the first time in Anglo-Saxon history, began their impossibly arduous two hundred mile march to York.

That same night all was quiet. Most of the men were asleep at the side of the road between London and York. There were those who couldn't sleep, and they stared dreamily into small campfires while listening to the occasional soft wings of the hunting owl.

Harold tied a small note onto the leg of a homing pigeon and released it. Silhouetted against the light of a September moon the pigeon raced toward the west, and then by an inexplicable force of nature it felt compelled to turn east and fly in the direction of Normandy.

Adelize lay tossing and turning in her bed. After a while she sensed something and sat up. Was that the fluttering of wings? She had imagined this sound several times a day, but this time she thought that she could see a pigeon walking back and forth on the balcony sill of the castle wall. Yes, this time it was not imagined. She stood, and very carefully approached the white pigeon; it was carrying a message. Her heart raced as she gently scooped up the pigeon and held it softly while untying the small note. She placed the pigeon back on the sill of the balcony and sat with her back to the light of the moon, and read these few words:

"At this moment my heart is a boundless flood of love and fear, my future queen. I think of you always. Harold."

The thin, weary, emaciated Adelize resumed her crying; the difference being that she didn't know now whether she was crying out of happiness or misery. She turned and stared in the direction of the channel, where her father was preparing to fight Harold, and she asked her god aloud once more, as she had done numerous times in the recent past, why this was happening? What earthly reason could explain this uncanny, bizarre, and inexplicable turn of fate that the two men in her life that she most loved and admired were now sworn to be the master of one another's destruction? She begged once more for a heavenly force to intervene, for certainly there was no earthly force in the known world that was anywhere close to being powerful enough to stop these two warrior-kings from a collision so colossal that the western world would forever be transformed by it.

There was a new chill in the late September air. Fall was forcing out the final days of summer in exactly the same manner that her father was trying to force Harold out of AngleLand. She spent the rest of the night lying on the stone-cold balcony floor without a blanket and with her long blonde hair laid over her eyes to block out a moon that was icy, unfriendly, and distant in every way. She had never felt so lost, and so alone.

That is how Matilda found Adelize two days later. The note was still clutched in her hand.

CHAPTER XXV

St. Valery

ON A HILLTOP NEAR THE statue of St. Valery, William, his generals, his half- brother Odo, and General Loutrec were having a heated discussion that at times seemed to walk the edge of an argument.

Behind them hundreds upon hundreds of long boats were moored off the Normandy coast. The night was closing in and as far as the eye could see in either direction there were thousands of troops along the seacoast that were grouped in clusters with campfires raging.

William had launched the invasion prematurely due to an impatience that was considered maniacal by some. The consequence was that the fleet was blown back to the Norman coast near St. Valery. History would congratulate William, for being a man with boundless good fortune because of this and another incident – but at the time the players were not aware of this, so the differences heated up fast.

William saw General Odo as an incorrigible pessimist who never stopped complaining. Now that Odo had something real and actual to complain about, he had become, to William, unbearable. William began to silently review his need for his half-brother, who William fully admitted to himself that if it were not for an accident of nature of his being a blood relative, then he would never pay attention to this man.

"What did I tell you, William?" asked Odo, while leaning in closer to William. "The men are beginning to believe that there is a curse on this enterprise. They're ready to abandon it once more. You never listen to me -- maybe now you will!"

"Quiet Odo!" said William in a moderate voice. Odo turned his head away and crossed his arms, staring out to sea with an aching heart. He saw himself as the Cassandra of Normandy – a Greek prophet that was always right, but no one ever listened to. "It's the vilest of all curses," he thought to himself, while his right eye blinked uncontrollably.

General Loutrec was troubled by another larger question, which seemed to be gathering momentum with each passing day. "I think some of the men are beginning to wonder if this invasion is really sanctioned by the pope, since there is no south wind. Do you see an inconsistency here, William, my dear friend, when we all know that God could easily order a south wind, if he so desired?"

"Yes I do," replied William. "There *is* an inconsistency, as you say: If the pope is the man that he pretends to be, then he would convey to his master that a south wind was vital to the health of the European people – but he hasn't done that...or even worse, he has done that but his master paid him no mind because he knows that the messenger is an imposter."

Alarmed by this the general took a step back. After a moment he turned and stood next to Odo with his arms folded. Both the general and Odo stared out at sea, sharing identical feelings of being vastly under rated by the world around them.

LanFranc tried to reduce the evident heat by uniting them all once again, so he suggested an evening prayer. He stepped forward and asked that they all place their hands atop one another's and he would lead the short appeal to the heavens.

William turned to LanFranc. "Before we all clasp our hands and speak to the unseen voice in the sky please tell me what you think, LanFranc...is the pope really the man that he says he is? Or could it be that the pope is just one more fashionable druid -- ready to use his druid sorcery to advance his personal agenda? I truly wonder if that's the case, LanFranc."

LanFranc could not find the words, but only stared at William with an open mouth. William walked a short distance away and left them standing next to the statue of St. Valery. After a brief period of murmuring in low voices Odo, LanFranc, and the general turned and left, carefully picking their way down the stairs to the road below.

William was tormented. It's became more and more apparent that he was alone in the belief that the invasion could work; and he was also beginning to feel that the others, including Adelize and Matilda, were beginning to perceive him as nothing more than a glory-seeking madman who had finally overplayed his hand.

After a moment William looked up at the statue of St. Valery and studied her face, who at this moment of his great difficulty, seemed to have a level of understanding that exceeded all earthly things; William dropped to his knees and, deeply grieved, put his face in his hands. After a while he looked up once again at St. Valery. There was an invitation in her manner, but particularly in her eyes and the flow of her hands.

"This genius of a sculptor has done his work", he thought wryly to himself, still resisting an inclination that was burgeoning inside of him; but then he began to think that perhaps there was something else to this. He waited, staring silently at her, until he felt an inexplicable pull in her direction. He began quietly…and softly…in a voice and manner not heard by anyone in William's history except Matilda on the day that he proposed to her.

"Please forgive me, St. Valery. My heavenly father will not listen to me. Just tell him I need a south wind for one day only--and if I get it, I will build a huge structure in the land of the Anglish – and I will call it the Tower Of London in his honor. It's a promise. Please forgive me…and now….I'm very tired."

With that William curled up in a ball on the cold stones beneath St. Valery and quickly fell asleep.

At the base of the statue of St. Valery William was still curled up from the early morning cold. Suddenly William was roused from his sleep by the cheer of thousands. He raised his head and looked down the shoreline and saw his soldiers cheering wildly at the direction of the flags. There was a south wind --- and a strong one at that. William turned to St. Valery, and with immeasurable gratitude bowed his head and thanked her with his entire being.

He vaulted over the stairway, landed on the ground below, and sprinted down the dirt path to where his horse was being held and cared for by attendants. He mounted his horse at a run and charged at full speed up the coastline, picking up the banner for the Lion of Normandy and riding with the banner flying in the wind while shouting to the soldiers in his exhilaration, making sure that his soldiers knew of his presence, and that they finally understood that the winds of good fortune belonged to them – and most importantly, that God was on their side after all.

The Lion of Normandy

The invasion had finally been blessed with a south wind. The roar of thousands shook the Norman coast as they watched William, one of the finest of all horse-men; demonstrate not just his prowess as a horseman, but his courage as an individual. For a man nearing forty he was as rugged and as daring as any man amongst them, which he was not shy about demonstrating whenever possible.

On this day he charged his horse straight for the sandy surf at a full gallop, stood straight up on its back, and when the horse slammed into the surf William flew straight over the horse's head and did a full layout somersault into the surf, soon emerging with a huge smile on his face, and throwing back his head with his arms spread wide and laughing a laugh that could be heard above the crashing of the waves and the roar of the approval of his soldiers.

This of course, was the kind of antics he was so well known for in the his untamed youth – but the Lion of Normandy was still very much perceived by all as a wild and youthful man that had no fear.

Soon the military cadre was gathered around William. Still wet from head to toe he made sure that his military understood that the day would be spent loading only the absolutely essential supplies; and reminded his generals to sort through the horses, making sure that only the hardiest and most well behaved were allowed to board the long ships for the night ride to the island – which could become treacherous in an instant because of the strength and unpredictability of the post-equinox south wind.

He paid particular attention to his archers: Recently they'd had plenty of time to hone their skills with William's new weapon – the long bow. The forests of yew trees had been reduced to near nothing in the area of Rouen as a result of this mandate. "But no worry," William told his generals, "Angle Land would have plenty of yew trees and they would all be theirs within a short time."

And finally he instructed the captain of each vessel to pay close attention to the unique light of "The Mora", the name of his boat, which would lead the eight hundred warships across the channel. The Mora was a gift from Matilda. It was made in her native country, Flanders, and was easily distinguished at night from the rest because of the reddish hue of the lantern. The Mora would guide the massive fleet to their destination, which was marked by reconnaissance on the south shore and known by mariners as Pevensey Bay. The invasion would be timed for the earliest light.

CHAPTER XXVI

The Battle of Stamford Bridge

THE VIKINGS WERE HARD AT work and had already lashed a log foundation together for this fort and trading center near York on the river Ouse. Hardrada was not a man who was afraid of physical labor; on the contrary he seemed to celebrate it; he and several men lifted another log on top of the foundation, and then stood back and critically examined it not just for function, but aesthetically as well. Tostig sat several yards away, assuring all that he would help if it wasn't for a back problem that came and went without warning.

Suddenly from a distance came a chorus of many yells and screams. The Vikings looked up from their work and in the direction of York. There were more screams. A moment later two riders, DireWulf and Lars rode into the Viking camp and dismounted. DireWulf, a seasoned warrior with part of his skull and one ear missing, struck a balance between calm and urgency.

The Anglish Dragon

"The Anglish are here! Huge columns, flying the dragon, their weapons glistening like ice in the morning sun."

"How far and how many?" asked Hardrada as Lothgar and others began surrounding DireWulf.

"A quarter-of-a-mile from York, and the numbers... it's hard to say...about the same as ours, maybe."

Hardrada slowly turned and stared at Tostig. "Tostig, come here now!"

Tostig was slightly shaken by this recent development. He limped over to them, mindful that the condition of his back was still under observation by the others.

"I thought you said that your brother, King Harold and his troops, was moving south from London and preparing for the south shore invasion."

"That's the information that I received, and that information came from my dear friend, Duke William himself," said Tostig, his voice cracking.

"You must think we're idiots. No army can march two hundred miles in four days--that's fifty miles a day over muddy roads while carrying their helmets, shields and swords," said Lothgar.

"I have fought all over the world, Tostig," exclaimed an angry Hardrada. "I have fought in Greece, Constantinople, Palestine, Rome, and no army can march that far, that fast! It can't be done!"

"It's physically impossible. It doesn't add up," said Lothgar.

"I tell you what adds up, Tostig. We have been set up," said Hardrada. "You are in on this with your brother Harold. Nothing else makes sense!"

Tostig began shaking. His eyes grew moist and his voice broke several times, but finally he said, "They are supposed to be fighting William on the south shore – I was just there with Duke William and Matilda, as their guest at Rouen, drinking mead and talking of the good times ahead. He is a personal friend of mine, and he is the one that recommended that you and I –"

But his voice was cut short by Hardrada as he picked Tostig up by the throat and lifted him off the ground with one arm. "You're a lying traitor, Tostig!"

Hardrada threw Tostig to the ground and turning to DireWulf, ordered him to pillory Tostig. DireWulf grabbed Tostig by the feet and dragged him away while Tostig screamed and thrashed about for mercy. Hardrada immediately conferred with his generals.

"They did not march two hundred miles from London to York in four days, because that's impossible! But whatever the true distance is, they will have to rest and regroup into battle formations before they think about challenging our eight thousand fighters, who have rested for several days now – so now is the time, while the Anglish are tired and hungry, their feet blistered, their muscles weary."

Lothgar agreed. "Tostig probably had the Anglish posted thirty miles south, but still thirty miles is a long way to walk before a fight. They are at their most vulnerable now. The sooner we attack them, the better."

Hardrada nodded, "But first I will talk to their new king, Harold Godwinson. If something is not worked out with this new king, then we'll wipe them out and take the whole island, north and south."

"Why talk? We should do that anyway. It's a perfect way of deciding who should be king of this land," said Lothgar.

Hardrada answered that while the talks were going on between the two sides all Vikings were to quietly become battle ready and positioned for a sudden and lethal strike straight to the heart of the Anglish." Lothgar saw this strategy and welcomed it.

King Harold, sitting atop Spanish Dancer, walked at the head of his troops as they moved past the village of York and toward Stamford Bridge. The citizens of York greeted the Anglish with both sides, shouting "Liberators...liberators...long live our King Harold... God be with our king...our liberator..." Some of the women were running alongside the troops carrying baskets of food with tears streaming down their faces, but the soldiers never broke stride as they marched straight through the town and toward Stamford Bridge.

When the Vikings were first sighted by the Anglish both sides began forming battle lines.

Hardrada could not believe that any leader could be so foolish as to fight without a rest – even if the distance were only thirty or so miles. "This King Harold must be completely out of his mind!" said Hardrada to the others.

After a short conference with his cadre King Harold mounted his horse. This was a signal that the negotiations between the leaders were about to begin.

Hardrada started to mount his horse, but because of his hulking size a stirrup broke and the horse spun a wild circle. Embarrassed by this, Hardrada took a running leap and flew on top of his horse. It reared and took several steps on its hind legs, and then Hardrada pranced on his horse toward the center of the plains for negotiations.

The Anglish Dragon versus the Viking Raven

Lothgar and DireWulf walked by his side. But Hardrada stopped some twenty yards away from Harold. He and his men signaled to Harold that they were close enough, and the negotiations could take place from this distance. King Harold didn't understand this, and neither did any of his men, but they were soon to learn why.

King Harold discovered that the reason that Hardrada stopped some twenty yards away to negotiate on the field with Harold was this:

Hardrada knew himself to be an engaging and colorful personality. Over the years he had learned that he could win over the sentiments of the soldiers with his antics, even from the side of the enemy, so he stood some distance from Harold so that they would be forced to speak in a manner that could be heard by the soldiers on both sides. Hardrada, because of his powerful voice and manner, and his ability to play the crowd on either side, knew from his vast experience that this had always put him at an advantage prior to the battle, and in some instances a battle had been avoided altogether.

Harold stared across at the well-known and notorious warrior-king of Norway, Hardrada, who he had heard about since he was in his late-teens. They nodded and smiled at one another. King Harold spoke first.

"What's wrong with Norway – too many Norwegians?"

Hardrada smiled a wide and engaging smile as he replied, "Nothing grows there...and I'm tired of eating fish. I'd like to include a few vegetables in my diet. Look at all this nice land to grow food on."

"This land isn't yours!"

"Whose land is it? You say it's yours...how did you come by it, Anglish Man?"

King Harold held up his battle-axe. "With this!" There were laughs from the Anglish.

"I have one, too…" Hardrada held up his battle-ax. "And I know how to use it. Why don't you and I settle this thing by ourselves…just you and me?"

"I'm too smart for that," answered Harold, with a hint of a smile.

Hardrada turned and shouted for all on both sides to hear, "We'll give your weary soldiers a rest while you and I fight to somebody's death…either yours or mine…let Odin decide the outcome." Hardrada threw back his head and laughed while pointing to the Anglish soldiers and bellowing in their direction,

"Would the weary Anglish like to have a rest after their long and grueling march, while watching their leaders decide the outcome? Tell me that you wouldn't like that, Anglish men! You know that you would, so let the North Man show you how to drink and feast, while you watch your leaders wrestle in the mud!"

The Vikings laughed and cheered. This was classic Hardrada. It was clear to all that they loved their leader.

"And after the outcome is decided by Odin, we will all feast and drink in the Viking way for weeks to come. Let us be your hosts, Anglish men!"

To Harold's dismay he could see that it wasn't just the Viking soldiers that were intrigued by this suggestion, but even some of his own men were becoming dangerously charmed by this charismatic man; and after their soon-to-be legendary two hundred mile march from London, who wouldn't find these suggestions attractive?

But just then there was a loud cheer from the Vikings as a pair of ravens flew on their right. Hardrada pointed them out with his axe.

"Odin's ravens, Thought and Memory fly on the right! It's a good omen for us – and a terrible one for the Anglish!" There was a loud cheer from the Vikings.

King Harold smiled, "Your horse ran away from you when you tried to mount it – always a sign of defeat. That's the omen that we will pay attention to, Hardrada!" The Anglish cheered and pounded their shields with their swords.

Hardrada smiled and nodded. After a while he asked, "Well let me ask you this--how much land will you give up to insure your peace, and also as citizens of this fine island, to guarantee that we fight your fights, as well as ours?"

With this, King Harold uttered his historically famous reply,

"For you Hardrada, just enough to bury you--about six feet!"

Hardrada took a moment before replying, but his reply left no doubt as to his decision. His deep chest effortlessly thundered these words for all of the Anglish to hear,

*Harold (Hard Rule) Hardrada,
warrior/king of Norway 1066*

"So be it! Then old Haarald Hardrada shall once again leave many bones behind to glut the wolves and the ravens of this fair land as the Anglish shall soon feel the might of the Hammer of Thor!"

Both of the warrior-kings nodded, turned slowly and in a crisp gallop rode back to their troops. It was then that Hardrada played his final card and brought out the hostage -- the King's brother, Tostig.

Tostig's head and hands were sticking through a wooden yoke while he was tied and bound in a sitting position on a horse. It was a strange contraption, and in all of Harold's war adventures he had never seen anything like it. Hardrada yelled to the Anglish side,

"We have your brother, Tostig, who collaborated with you. His life must be worth something. Think on it!"

"I have thought on it," was Harold's immediate response.

"What do you have to say?" asked Hardrada.

King Harold, after looks to the right, and then to the left, yelled "I say....CHARGE!"

The Anglish, after walking through the mud carrying sword and shield for two hundred miles -- without a rest after arriving at their destination-- charged the eight thousand undefeated Vikings of Hardrada's Norway.

On King Harold's words DireWulf rammed a spear through Tostig's chest, which protruded through his back. With a single blow from DireWulf's sword he sliced off the head of Tostig, and as it rolled across the ground he ran it down, picked it up, and stuck it on the spear that protruded from Tostig's back. The head had been piked on the spear.

DireWulf whacked the rear of the horse firmly with the flat of his sword; Tostig's horse made a frantic leap and bolted wildly; during the battle the horse could be seen galloping across the battlefield carrying the headless pilloried torso of Tostig with his head piked on his back. No more ghastly sight could be imagined.

The Vikings and the Anglish met in the center of the plains with both sides fighting heroically and ferociously. Hardrada could be seen spinning on his horse, knocking the Anglish through the air with a single blow. King Harold was knocked off Spanish Dancer and was fighting on his feet.

Much time had passed and the field was strewn with bodies. The glory of battle was now seen as a nightmarish dream that could not possibly be real, with amputees wandering in a trance without arms; there were howls of pain, with people slipping and falling because of the amount of blood underfoot – and essentially the wreckage and carnage of war was seen for what it really was.

Lothgar and DireWulf sprinted for all they were worth with their battle-axes raised. To them, no matter could possibly be more urgent. The reason for their horror was that they arrived at the fatally wounded body of Norway's hero, Haarald Hardrada. Hardrada had a severe axe wound to the chest. Lothgar held up his brother's head, watching as his brother Haarald Hardrada sprayed blood as he spoke his final words.

"I have heard the voices of the Valkyries and felt their soft wings brush past. Please take me home."

Lothgar and DireWulf, their hearts bursting with emotion, immediately signaled a truce. The battle of Stamford Shire Bridge was over.

King Harold II

King Harold walked over to Lothgar and DireWulf accompanied by several others and said, "You are free to go, but you must give me your word that you will never set foot on Anglish soil again."

Once Lothgar and DireWulf nodded their promises, they hoisted up the body of Hardrada with the help of several and carried him to his dragon boat. It was over. Eight out of ten Vikings were killed in that great battle. They barely had enough men left to navigate their boats back to Norway.

A while later the York villagers appeared. All tended to the wounded of Vikings and Anglish equally without taking sides. The Vikings had arrived with two hundred and forty dragon boats; and now there were only twenty-four of these war ships that were returning;

these were drifting with the current of the River Ouse loaded with the bodies of the warriors who had died in battle. That was the final Viking invasion into the Land of the Angles.

When the word traveled throughout the western world of Haarald Hardrada's death, all were impacted in their own way. The stone engraving at the site by the York villagers read,

HAARALD HARDRADA, KING OF NORWAY, WAS ALSO KING OF NORTH ENGLAND FOR ONE DAY.

September 20th of 1066 marked the last day of a Viking invasion of Angle Land.

CHAPTER XXVII

William and Adelize:

Their Sacred Promises

WHEN THE NEWS OF HARDRADA'S defeat and death reached William he had a quiet moment. It didn't matter to William in the slightest that he was distantly related to Hardrada, or that their Norwegian ancestors had once fought for the same causes under the same flag; it was the loss of a soldier that never asked anything of his men that he would not do himself. Hardrada, they had consistently said, never considered himself any more or any less than the rest of his men. He marched at their side, fought next to them, ate and drank with them, and worked with his hands right alongside them. He played the harp around the campfires in the evenings, and listened to their stories and laughed at their humor. William now felt personally responsible for suggesting to Tostig that he align with Hardrada. What William never counted on in a thousand years, and still did not fully believe was that King Harold of Angle Land would march that far and that fast to York, fight eight thousand fully rested Vikings, and defeat Hardrada. It still seemed absolutely impossible, and William still wondered if his messengers had gotten the news of this all wrong.

Like Hardrada's brother, Lothgar, William had calculated the physicality of the two hundred mile march in four days and the fighting of the undefeated Hardrada without a rest as simply being beyond the scope of rational belief. He wondered if this weren't a trap of some kind, set by King Harold. Were Harold's forces waiting just beyond Hastings, laying low and out of sight, ready to pounce on them while they were getting out of their boats? He had to be careful. Many of these messengers that showed up with news reports were nothing but lying dogs that could, with the snap of fingers, change their form into an unsavory vapor and disappear through a crack in the floor. Reconnaissance with trusted people and news sources was absolutely essential if a leader was to make the correct decisions. Bad information was the one thing that could turn all of his dreams and ambitions into a pile of rubble in a matter of minutes. He summoned a bevy of scouts and instructed them to go deep inland prior to the invasion and make sure that Harold Godwinson was not waiting just over a hill with ten thousand Anglish troops – waiting to turn the sky black with arrows as they were getting out of their boats. That was number one on the agenda.

As far as the death of Harold's brother, Tostig, William felt nothing at all. William had, however, secretly congratulated himself on the chess strategy of sending Tostig to join forces with Hardrada and pulling the Anglish King Harold north – away from the south shore – if the information proved to be correct. No one but Matilda had known about this. He intended to make sure that it stayed that way; otherwise there would be those individuals, and perhaps entire nations, that would hold William personally responsible for the death of Haarald Hardrada of Norway. Still, in a thousand lifetimes he could have never predicted this outcome – *if* it was true! William still had to see for himself before he would fully believe that Harold's physically impossible march and defeat of Hardrada had actually happened.

But, if it were true, and these messengers proved to be correct, then his old friend King Harold would never be able to cover the two hundred and seventy miles (as the crow flies) back from York to the island's south shore after the battle of Stamford Bridge. Not a chance! He and his soldiers would be lucky to get back to London after what they had been through, with half of his troops running away and disappearing into the forests of North Umbria for a better life on the return trip to London, and the other half collapsing from exhaustion. Nor did he have to worry about a volunteer military suddenly coming out of nowhere to defend the south shore, because all the able fighters around London had already volunteered and moved north to York. What able fighters would stay behind, for the exception of London's usual permanent guard, known as the HouseCarls? But now London was a bird's nest on the ground. Because of the totality of these things Duke William felt that God had made it clear that the invasion was blessed in every way, and that he, in fact, was blessed also.

But now he had a pounding headache from thinking about all of this. William watched as the last of the horses, some of which were recalcitrant troublemakers, boarded the long ships on heavy ramps.

He watched from his horse as his men put their backs to the dragon boats and launched the final ones from the shore through the use of rollers. Finally all boats had been launched and were in deep water except the Mora, which was anchored both stern and bow in shallow water with a ramp for William's horse. William had raised his sword high in the air and was about to give the command to the invasion fleet to "Hoist the mainsail" when he saw a lone rider approaching, the stature of which was keenly familiar to him, even though she was entirely covered.

William spurred his horse toward her, dismounted and helped her off of her horse. There was fire in the

blue green eyes of Adelize; but she was alarmingly un-
derweight, her hair was unwashed and tangled, and her
complexion was so bleached from being bed-ridden
that she was barely recognizable. She grabbed a stirrup
for support until she felt enough strength to continue,
all the while drilling her father with a lethal stare.

”Not one hair on his head shall be harmed, father.”

”Adelize, I have to leave. I love you with all of my
heart. Tell your mother—“

“I will not be satisfied, father, until I have your word
that no harm shall come to Harold.”

”This is war, Adelize, and I’m sorry but I can’t make
that promise.”

”You *can* make that promise!” said the emaciated
Adelize with a force that surprised William. “You are
taking a land that doesn’t belong to you, and a crown
that doesn’t belong to you--but that’s where it all ends!
The life of Harold does not belong to you--and you will
not take it!”

”These matters are highly complex, and have to do
with principle. You’re too young to understand.”

Adelize erupted with her final reserve of energy,
”Yes father, I guess that I’m too young to understand,
because when you speak of ‘principle’, I’m wondering
what principle you’re talking about? Are you speaking of the principles of Alexander and Julius Caesar,
who I learned from you were history’s most celebrated
black-hearted degenerates whose greatest thrill was to

watch hordes of people running before them, crying, screaming, and begging for their lives? I don't have to tell you that they slaughtered hundreds of thousands of people, because I learned these things from you – or have you forgotten?"

"I remember, but I think you're forgetting that I have eight hundred war ships waiting for me, Adelize--"

"Waiting for what? Waiting so that Normandy can kill men, rape women, and turn children into slaves like those two mentally-deranged monsters -- Alexander and Caesar?

"We will have this conversation, but it won't be now, Adelize. Now go to your mother! That's an order!"

"My mother left – she's in Flanders now; and I will leave this place also – so everything is yours! I despise it here, just like my mother, and just like your estranged sons, Robert and William. Oh, and I'm sorry for mentioning their names, father, I know that I'm not supposed to – but I will mention Harold's name, and I will say to you that if any harm comes to Harold then I can promise you, with all that I stand for in this life, that neither you or my mother will ever see me again."

William looked deep into her eyes and saw that his princess could not be more resolute on this matter.

"Adelize, you and your mother mean more to me than all the land in the world, and—"

"Father, I have heard that before and now is the time to put that to a test. No harm to Harold!"

After a moment William softly said to her,

"Alright Adelize, no harm shall come to Harold! That's my promise to you!"

Adelize, overcome by a dilemma the magnitude of which few people on this earth could ever experience, leaned forward into her father and placed her forehead on his chest. William hugged Adelize with both arms. This was the moment in the later years of his life that he would turn over and over in his memory. He remembered how after a short while the dam broke and her tears flowed unrestrained. He remembered that he had placed both his hands under her chin, tilted her face up, and putting the tip of his nose to hers quietly said, "Don't you worry, my beautiful princess Adelize. You know who I am by now, and I will protect your handsome king. And just know that in an odd way, Adelize, I haven't given up on the idea that we will all be a family of one someday. In fact, that's my secret hope. "

Maybe it was the angst in her eyes and the flow of her hands, but at this moment as he looked into the eyes of his daughter, William felt that she bore an uncanny resemblance to the statue that he had prayed to only the night before, St. Valery.

And of course his words to her were the precise words that she, not merely wanted to hear, but had to hear. He dried her eyes with the tips of his fingers and gently gave her several tiny kisses on her lips. Then

William turned to his fleet and yelled the command: "Hoist the mainsail!" The command was repeated a thousand times by his captains up and down the coast of Normandy, and the sails cracked like lightning and rolled like thunder as the wind snapped them to.

William turned back to his Adelize; he pulled her face into his chest and playfully tousled her hair while saying with a deep-felt heartiness,

"I have told myself more times than I could count that without you I would have no life at all. You are my greatest achievement, and I love you my sweet princess Adelize, with all of my heart...all of my heart...all of my heart!"

With this William gently turned from her and quietly climbed onto his warhorse. After a moment of smiling to her he suddenly leaped forward and was soon at a full gallop, hitting the surf and climbing the ramp to his dragon boat, The Mora. As a squire took his horse he turned and waved to Adelize from the bow as the huge warship moved north to Angle Land. She quietly waved back with what little strength she had and watched as William the Conqueror, with the sails of square-rigger bulging, tacked to the front and center of the invasion fleet.

The day was historical for Adelize, because it marked the first time in her life that she had seen tears flow freely from her father's eyes and roll down his cheeks.

The Mora

This part of the world was now losing its light. A gentle rain began to fall. Adelize stood in that spot on the Normandy shore without moving for a very long time, until she could no longer see a trace of the lantern with the reddish hue that marked the war ship with the smiling dragon on its prow that was leading the largest invasion of this island since Julius Caesar.

William, as he caught sight of her in the far distance, standing all alone without moving, felt that there was something holy about her, and that there was not a man in the world that was good enough for her -- except perhaps...Harold, King of north German tribes known as the Angles, Saxons, and Danes.

CHAPTER XXVIII

The Nordic Omen

HAROLD'S TROOPS WERE MASSING IN a column through the center of York. A beautiful lady of York and her two sisters, who would certainly tempt any man of lesser character, made an urgent appeal to Harold, who was war-torn and mounted on his horse.

"It simply is unthinkable for you and your men to march from London to here and fight the Vikings, and then without convalescing here with us, for a short time anyway, to march back to London. We simply cannot permit you, gracious King, to do such a thing."

"I'm sorry, my lady, but the south shore of our island is undefended. Our recovery must take place in London. Farewell, and thank you for your hospitality."

Harold raised his sword and gave the command to begin the impossibly long and grueling two hundred mile return march from York to London.

The soldiers, war-torn, wounded, ragged, many limping badly, started their long march home. Most of the soldiers had nothing but goat or sheep skin strips wrapped around their feet and pulled tightly around their ankles. That was the extent of their 'long march apparel', and not much else. The villagers of York cheered their heroes wildly as they moved out to the beat of the drums of the local marching band. Within an hour Harold's troops had disappeared over a distant hill from the sight of the villagers.

On the Norwegian coast the sky was a swirling mass of black, gray, and white clouds, serving as a tempestuous canopy for the man that lived a full and turbulent life, Haarald Hardrada.

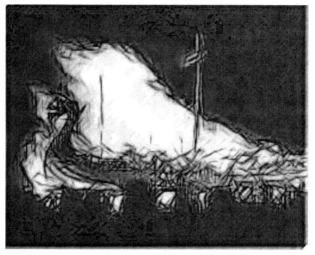

Hardrada's ride to Valhalla

The Vikings chanted their farewells as Hardrada's dragon boat bursts into flames just off the coast. Suddenly some of the Vikings pointed to the sky and yelled to the others,

"It's Odin! Odin! Odin!"

In the sky the fiery clouds of smoke had formed a shape that could have easily been interpreted as the face of the one-eyed Odin with his winged-helmet. Lothgar was standing with his Norse maidens and was transfixed by this image, saying to DireWulf "It's a sign, DireWulf, that the sky shall rain the blood of a great battle."

"Aye, Lothgar!" nodded DireWulf, "and the battle is soon to come."

No sooner did he say these words then the lightning cracked, the thunder rolled, and it began to rain.

The Vikings did not seek shelter, but instead opened their arms to the sky and celebrated their great leader's journey to Valhalla; the place where all felt confident that they would be taken to by the Nordic angels known by them as theValkyries to re-unite with him and the other heroes of the north someday, should they die heroically on the field of battle, as the valiant warrior of the north, King Haarald (Hard Rule) Hardrada had.

CHAPTER XXIX

London learns of the Norman landing

IT WAS SUNRISE ON THE south coast of Angle Land. A south wind had driven the Normans straight to their destination, Pevensey Bay. William's reconnaissance, who had been prowling the hills and ravines on the south shore for weeks, had descended the steep terrain and had met The Mora. They gave an exuberant William the all clear signal.

On the 28th of September 1066 a.d. William and his fleet gave thanks to the heavens that there were not hordes of Anglish men waiting to blacken the sky with arrows and cut down the invaders as they tried to get out of their boats. William took time to make it clear to his men that this was indisputable evidence that God was on their side. He leaped from the boat and landed knee deep in shallow water, but slipped and fell backward. Virtually all smiles vanished. For the descendants of the Norse, this was the most horrible of all omens – stumbling on the ground to be won; but

William recovered immediately, and with great charisma and a winning smile, held dirt in both of his hands and yelled to the discomfited witnesses his historically famous remark:

"By the splendor of God I have already seized the earth of Angle Land in my two hands!"

The smiles returned, and finally all laughed and applauded. More Normans began jumping from their shallow running dragon boats and splashing in the surf, and some went so far as to imitate William, digging the earth up with their two hands and holding it triumphantly overhead.

Horses began to disembark on ramps, and within a very short time the south shore was garrisoned by Normans.

———◆———

The city of London had never heard bells ring with such joy as when Harold's troops were spotted on a distant hill marching toward London. Who were these returning Anglish heroes that had done the impossible and defeated Haarald Hardrada in the far north? All soldiers would be regaled with the finest of medics and the greatest comfort that could possibly be bestowed upon returning troops. The town would spare no expense in letting their warriors know just how grateful they were. As the war-torn heroes arrived the air was filled with shrieks, screams, muffled sobs, and Harold was virtually surrounded with as much adulation as a single individual had ever experienced since this town's inception.

Yet Harold was troubled. He had noticed that the flags that were flying from the towers were all pointed north. The wind had been gentle at first, and then had augmented noticeably just outside of London. Before he did so much as take a drink of water he had to make sure that fresh riders were dispatched to the south shore to give a full and detailed report. King Harold, surrounded by palace guards, slowly and painfully dismounted. After a moment he weaved, his eyes lost focus, and out of sheer exhaustion he fell to the ground like a piece of timber.

Within the King's Palace Harold was carefully tended to by doctors. Bishop Verser and other noblemen were present. Harold had been unconscious for several days, and it was apparent by the doctor's questions that he had just opened his eyes:

"Do you know where you are?" Harold looked around the room and answered that he did. The doctor asked Harold who this particular man was, and if he knew him. Harold answered that the man was Bishop Verser. Harold was asked who he was, and he answered without hesitation that he was the king of the greatest of all nations. The doctor turned to Bishop Verser and said that Harold would probably have a full recovery if he did not move from his bed unless absolutely necessary, and if he judiciously followed the prescribed recommendations by the medical staff and further noted that the leeches had been taken from their fine mesh pens in the castle pond, blessed by the appropriate people, and were at this very moment in transport.

Harold listened to this talk and was a little taken aback by it. He remembered clearly dismounting from his horse, and that seemed to be only several minutes ago. He was surprised to learn that it was days ago that he had ridden into London and, along with his soldiers, received a hero's welcome from every single one of London's eighteen thousand inhabitants; he also learned that he had collapsed from exhaustion and still had a fever. Harold was thirsty and asked for a drink of water, which he immediately received. After taking the drink of water as all silently watched, he sat it down and turned to Bishop Verser, asking him if there was a south wind. Bishop Verser reluctantly answered that the wind had been blowing from the south for several days. Harold asked the Bishop if the Normans had landed. The Bishop hesitated for no more than a second and that was all that Harold needed to see; he sat straight up, and when he was descended on by all in the

room he shouted at them with what little breath he had
left and ordered them to back away.

Everyone complied except for Bishop Verser, who
was trying desperately to get Harold to lie back down;
but Harold in no time had broken free and was already
getting dressed. The Bishop vigorously protested, but
Harold reminded him that he was the king now and
subject to no one's demands but his own.

Within minutes he was partially dressed and making his way down the palace hallway while putting on
the rest of his clothes, ordering that Spanish Dancer
be readied, and that the bells were to toll, and that all
available armed personnel would gather in the square
outside the palace to begin the march to the south
shore. The doctors looked toward Bishop Verser for
help, knowing in advance that he was just as power-
less to stop Harold as they were, but still thinking that
the Bishop might have some secret card to play. While
mulling their strategy regarding these things they were
close to tears. Never before had they seen such a stubborn, recalcitrant, hard-headed, tenacious, obstinate
and wonderfully heroic King, both in presence and in
deed.

They went looking for Harold and learned that he
had asked to be taken to the blacksmith's quarters by
the palace guards; and so Angle Land's royalty, out of
urgency, gathered strength in numbers while searching him out, secretly hoping that when they found him

he would collapse out of exhaustion once more and go into a coma again so that he would be far easier to manage.

Everyone knew that Bishop Verser was loved and respected by Harold as no other man on the island, so they turned to him for insight into their new king:

Bishop Verser intimated that their new king was like one of the knights of the Welsh King's round table (all Anglish and Normans were enamored by the campfire tales of the fifth century king known as Arthur of Wales); Harold, like an Arthurian knight, would heroically fight any kind of monster without hesitation, respected wealth but was not motivated by it; loved and respected women at all times; fought under the sign of the Questing Beast; and unquestionably his true religion was "honor" – and for him that amounted to the idea that a man should always do the right thing – whether god was watching or not. Above all else Harold often stated that he was the sworn enemy of deceit, lies and hypocrisy, and Harold had more than once said that he would like to be remembered as "The man that could not be bought!"

But if Harold had a fault, he said, it was that he could not coldly detach himself from events or people. He had a strong mind, but an even stronger heart, and his heart almost always ruled his mind; but a strategist, he reminded them, must let his mind rule his heart; his mind must make the decisions while his heart provides the energy to carry out those decisions, and then he gave an example of such a man -- and that man was William, the Duke of Normandy. "William, like a chess player, was a brilliant strategist, and William seldom, like a chess player, let his heart get in the way of any decision."

All listened to the bishop with a heightened interest. Everything he had said was very consistent with their known history of Harold and had made perfect sense to them. At that moment they saw two palace guards rushing towards them. Harold had collapsed while talking to the blacksmiths. This was possibly good news, they thought; now their king would finally be subjected to a forced convalescing.

Several days later Harold seemed to have recovered much of his physical strength. More importantly Harold had come to his senses and had now realized that he could no longer simply will himself to physically perform the way that he would like to perform.

Harold now had time to thoughtfully examine the findings of the reconnaissance, and that information told Harold that William, while not moving inland yet, was using his combat forces on the south shore to protect the greater portion of his supply chain as they landed.

The reasoning behind this was to become firmly established with a military that was massive and functioning in every way -- as opposed to one that was damaged, cold, hungry, and scattered – like his own.

It was William's assessment of the Anglish that the fighting core of Harold's troops could barely walk, and they probably were not going to try to march a severely grueling seventy miles to the south shore to fight a rested, combat ready William and his massive Norman forces. A more likely prospect would be that Harold would allow his troops to recover in London, where they had beds, medical attention, food, water, and all the necessary requirements for a speedy recovery.

Furthermore the idea of defending London, where Harold's troops had a defense infrastructure already in place, would be far more attractive to his troops than marching to the south shore with nothing but hope in their hearts and setting up some kind of tortoise defense with their shields – surely Harold wouldn't do that!

But William was wrong. He learned that Harold had put together several thousand troops and was marching the seventy miles from London to the south shore to drive away the Norman forces.

William, when he heard the news, only shook his head and asked, "What the **** is this man thinking?" But at the same time he was comforted by the news; Harold's defeat would be made much easier when his troops showed up, weary and exhausted, with only a tortoise-shell defense standing between him and the conquest of the Land of the Angles.

———◆———

A mounted Harold was leading his troops from London to the south shore to a place near Hastings. The turnout was small. Harold had sent several of his officers out to get an estimate, but he knew from experience that the count was nowhere near the count that he had when he fought Hardrada. He lost a lot of men in that battle, and many more defected into the forests of North Umbria on the way back, not because they were cowards or slackers, but because they were good men who could not go any further. If they were slackers they would not have marched to York to fight Hardrada's undefeated in the first place. Most of the ones that had finally made it back to London were determined to stay in London – no more demanding long marches to fight professional soldiers who were completely armed and rested – and waiting for them. Their minds did not make these decisions – their thoroughly exhausted and spent bodies had made it for them.

Harold's troops soon came to the conclusion that if every man was an uber-man like Harold himself, then they could do the things that he was asking of them. But they weren't. They were not gods – they were ordinary men who were trying to defend a country that they loved, and they had vowed to give everything that they had – and that's exactly what they had done. They had given it all, and they had nothing left – or so it seemed.

CHAPTER XXX

Verser the Varangian

BISHOP VERSER WAS BEYOND DESPAIRING; he was close to being a broken man. He had watched with sorrow in his heart as his best friend Harold had tried to pull everything together and once again fire the engine of war. Harold left London with only a smattering of forces that would be necessary to even hold the line on the south shore. The bishop was near tears for the first time since his soldiering with the Varangians.

The Sign of the Varangian Guard

The bishop had a history that very few knew about. He was far more complex than anyone could possibly imagine. Only Harold and a few others knew of the bishop's early life as a warrior that came as a dark and terrible storm out of a country that was located in a mountainous region on the southern side of the Alps near a village known as Vienna. He had a name then, and it was not Bishop Verser. Verser first fought as a Swiss mercenary; the problem was that they really were mercenaries, who swore allegiance only to gold – so he left them and moved on. From there he fought with the Kelts of Brittany, and then the Norse of Normandy. From Norse Land he sailed with his fellow Norse to an island in the middle of nowhere that was nothing more than an ice sheet stretched over a rock. It was called Iceland. Verser described his Icelandic days as the happiest days of his life, but he lost his family there in a dispute with a grandson of Eric the Red. Following that a cloud of darkness blacked out the sun in his life and never left. He said goodbye to Iceland and traveled to the land of a north German tribe known as the Swedes, where he signed up to travel east with the Swedish Vikings, sometimes known as the Varangians.

The Varangians were Vikings that traveled east, usually down the Dnieper River. He quickly distinguished himself as a man that left nothing standing in his wake; he became a dark and terrible force that swept through Russia all the way to the Byzantine Empire.

He had become well known, and soon he had an invitation to become part of the elite guard of the Byzantine Empire. Once there he decided to visit the famed cathedral known as *the Hagia Sophia.*

Interior: The Hagia Sophia of Constantinople

While walking in a circle and staring up at a ceiling so magnificent that only the gods could have designed it, he had an attack of some kind which came as a direct result of viewing the splendor of the heavenly structure. The Varangian collapsed on the floor of the massive cathedral and had to convalesce in Constantinople for several weeks. During this time he acquainted himself with the biblical writings of the ancients. The continuing problem, though, was that he would, unprovoked, burst into tears without apparent cause, and this would profoundly embarrass him. He left the guard and vowed never to fight again. After his recovery he wandered on foot for years, moving through the Alps, a brief stay in Paris, and then wandered across the sea to the island known by some as Ireland. It was in Dublin, founded by the Vikings, that he renewed his interest in the written word of the ancients.

From there he traveled the short distance to Angle land where he visited a sacred place of the Kelts known as Stonehenge. He spent weeks sleeping on the ground there and examining the megaliths, trying to figure out where these stones came from, how they were transported there, how they were placed, and what exactly did they mean? He conferred with the druids on this matter for a time, but came to the conclusion that there were certain things, like lightning and thunder, rainbows, the movement of a cloud of starlings, the directional mechanisms of homing pigeons, or even the

amazing acrobatic flight of a dragonfly that would always baffle him. It was during his time in this land that
he officially became a monk in a monastery in West
Saxony, later to be known as Wessex.

Soon his thoughts and manner were highly revered
wherever he went. He became a confidant of King
Edward the Confessor. It was during that time that he
became a bishop. He watched as the Godwinson family
challenged Edward the Confessor, and he found himself appointed as a mediator in the conflict between
the Godwinson family and Edward. It was highly unusual for a mediator to be well respected by both sides,
but both sides had recognized that Bishop Verser was a
man who was a born slave to the meaning of the word
"honor". It was then that he, along with Edward, saw
that the Godwinson family had an extraordinarily
gifted son who had become an adventurer, a carouser, a jouster, a fighter, and an academic. They all saw
great potential with Harold Godwinson; they felt that
within Harold an extraordinary leader of his people
slumbered; but Harold wanted no part of royalty. Most
of the rumors about Harold were true, and that's why
the rumors persisted for so long; but lying dormant
inside of him was an unquestionable potential for
greatness, which many had seen and recognized. So,
Bishop Verser and Harold Godwinson over time had
become trusted friends, and they were still lifelong
and trusted friends, and this is why the Bishop found

that tears were flowing freely and involuntarily down his face for the first time since he had collapsed on the floors of the Hagia Sophia while a commander of the Varangians and a member of the elite guard of the Byzantine Empire.

But the bishop's day had arrived. After the bell's had tolled furiously throughout London, and the word had spread that Bishop Verser was going to offer his resignation at noon, there arrived a crowd that London had seldom seen; there was a sea of angry faces as far as the eye could see; almost all were "mired in ire", as some said, to protest Bishop Verser's defection in this time of crisis. They were ready to let him have it when he showed his face to the crowd. When the bishop finally arrived there was a roar of anger that shook London to its foundations. The bishop stood front and center with his arms folded and waited for the crowd to lose its voice. After a lengthy time the bishop raised both hands, and the crowd finally calmed so that they could hear the bishops feeble explanation, whatever it was.

After a while he spoke with a surprising resonance; the buildings of London provided a natural amphitheater for him, so he was easily heard by the throngs of Londoners; and without a trace of castigation, the bishop said these words to the citizens of London:

"Hear the words of this old knight, my friends, whose battle scars are as many and as deep as any man's

living, and who has, at this moment, come out of retirement to fight once again. Now, will you let the North
Man invaders rape your sisters and your wives, behead
your sons and steal your homes and your lands?

    And will you let our King Harold, the greatest king
this newborn nation has ever had, walk down the road
to Hastings by himself and meet the Norman invaders
alone? We will all die someday--nobody escapes that!
Then why not die for a sacred cause, a hallowed cause,
so that when our time comes we can rejoice in the kingdom of heaven with our loved ones and with a clear
conscience, rather than snivel through an afterlife in
the place of the damned, in the place of Tostig, and
other traitors and cowards?"

    Bishop Verser removed his monk's robe and tossed
it to a nearby monk. The monk gasped, but his gasp
was not heard because of the huge vocal response of
the crowd, which was teetering in open-mouthed disbelief. Bishop Verser, a man now in his early fifties, still
had the countenance, the muscle tone, and the presence of a gladiator; but it was the deep purple scars
that ran lengthwise on his legs and torso, and the red
scars that were formerly puncture wounds on his arms,
shoulders, and chest, that caused the crowd to suddenly quiet; or perhaps it was his head, normally covered
by his monk's robe and now in plain view that was revealed as a horrific mass of scar tissue. During his days
as a Varangian these scars were seen as things of beauty

by his fellow warriors; but to this crowd, nothing could be more frightening than to see a man of the cloth reveal himself in this manner; and now this holy man was easily juggling a battle axe and a sword, without taking his eyes off of the crowd, as he had done with his fellow Vikings on the long trips down the Dnieper River while coasting with the current on the dragon boats to thwart boredom. That was in the old days. He had done this for hours and hours in his youth, but today the juggling of axe and sword was not to thwart boredom. Far from it! Today it had a special significance.

"The hearts of all Anglish men and women are on trial today. Who of you will join me, and who of you will join what may very well be the last native king of Angle Land, our King Harold, to defend everything that we love, everything that we stand for? Where's your hearts, lads? Is it so terrible to choose the time that you die--and the way that you die? Come with me lads, let's join our king!"

And with that the Varangian known as Verser slid the chain mail over his head, and picked up the sword, which he held up high in front of the crowd. The crowd of Angles, Danes, Saxons, and Kelts thundered their approval, for on this day they were all one.

As the bishop walked down the stairs and through the crowd the people were overwhelmed and parted a path for him. He began the long walk to Hastings, and all that could make the journey joined 'Verser the

Varangian'. Many of them weren't professional soldiers; some of them had never held a weapon in their life. There were numerous males that were only adolescents barely in their teens – but they could draw a bow as well as any man, and some of the volunteers were women that were sworn to tend to the wounded on the battle-field and die right next to their soldiers, should that be their destiny. Once the recovering soldiers in London who had fought Haardrada at York heard about this new development with the bishop, they struggled to get to their feet and make the journey to the south shore no matter what. If they had to crawl on their hands and knees on the old Roman road to the great battle, then so be it! They would not be left behind while their women and young men were fighting in their place.

But perhaps the greatest significance of Verser's speech was the recruiting of the HouseCarls. They were an elite force of extremely fit, infinitely coura-geous and well-trained fighters that were the guardians of the city while the troops were away. The HouseCarls saw that their time had come, and that there would be no London to guard if the Normans were not stopped, so most of the HouseCarls did the unthinkable -- leav-ing their post in London and joining the Varangian in the march to Hastings.

King Harold was walking at the head of his columns on the old Roman road to Hastings and conferring with several of his men when he heard the sound of voices coming from behind them in the very far distance. His men had heard the voices also and had slowed their step to a near halt. The voices over time became more and more distinct. Finally, rising over the nearest hill, he saw several regiments of Anglish soldiers marching toward them and singing their favorite marching song.

King Harold had seen a lot in his lifetime, but at this moment his heart was bursting with emotion. Ashamed of his moist eyes, he hid his face from his men as he turned to Spanish Dancer, who had been walking behind him, and climbed on top of him. Harold's first command was to have the cadre spread the word amongst the troops that they were to camp on this spot for the night so that the generals could confer regarding the new troop force.

The troops spread out and soon campfires were lit on both side of the road as able bodies stomped through the woods for firewood, hunters were dispatched for game, and others went with containers to nearby springs to fetch water. They moved quickly so that the new arrivals would be welcomed into a functioning camp where most of the work was already done, and they could see for themselves the joy and appreciation that Harold's soldiers had for the new recruits.

Harold stood at the center of the road to welcome this grey haired warrior walking toward him front and center, wearing chain mail with sword and shield at the head of the new recruits. But just who in the hell was this man, he asked Gyrth -- but Gyrth had no idea?!

Soon though, he recognized the man as the greatest friend that any man could ever have, Bishop Verser. The Varangian had come out of retirement. What words could a son possibly have for a father who demonstrated such love for god, family, and country? There weren't any, so Harold found that he could only walk toward him and wordlessly wrap his arms around him and crush him endlessly with a mighty bear hug. There were smiles and tears everywhere, and it was nearly forgotten that within a matter of a day or so there would be a battle so great that many that were beneath this rising moon would never see one another again. But enough, they thought, and so they prepared their weapons and armor around the campfires.

Harold amazed all with his famous Tawny owl calls in answer to a lonely female Tawny owl. There was a back and forth for a short while that excited all listeners, but it turned out to be his brother Gyrth, who had hidden in the woods and was only pranking him as he had done a thousand times before in his youth.

But soon things became serious as the stars made their appearance. The reconnaissance had set what was to become known after this battle as Senlac Hill as the most viable place to make their stand. Their troops were tired, the Normans troops were entirely fresh, so the strategy was to place themselves at the top of the hill and hope that the Normans wore themselves out trying to charge uphill over and over in an attempt to break the line. The defense would also incorporate the Macedonian line of overlapping shields, sometimes known as the "tortoise shell defense".

They would, of course, position their best knights on the flank to prevent the Norman knights from making their flanking movements in an attempt to circle behind the Anglish and attack from behind. If that happened then the Anglish defense would quickly fall apart.

More than anything, because of the comparatively weak troop strength, combined with the lack of experience of many, plus the exhausted soldiers from the recent battles, the effort was to be entirely defensive until there was a tangible change in their favor, and then, like a chess strategist laying out a basic design, they would play it moment to moment within that framework. This was the defense model that Verser, Harold, Gyrth, and several of the generals agreed upon.

Gyrth added that the future had arrived at the doorstep of the Anglish, and soon all would discover that destiny had put Normandy on the scaffold for their crimes of invading a free land. Each took a sip of mead from their leather vessels and celebrated the words of Gyrth.

In closing the bishop led a short prayer, and then, as an improvised continuation the bishop said:

"Because I have, in my long life, dear Lord, seen too many times when darkness prevailed over light – and when wrong prevailed over right – and it is because of this that we are hoping and praying that the great fiery light of 1066 that streaked across the sky earlier this year and passed over this blessed island of ours was none other than your holy messenger known to us as "Winged Victory" and that this was your sign to us that she would be standing with us on the field during the great battle tomorrow, and see that the Anglish Dragon defeats forever the Lion of Normandy! That is our prayer, dear Lord. Amen!"

All repeated the word "Amen!" before adjourning to their individual sleeping quarters. Each laid their heads down to rest, and rest only, for there was no such thing as sleep; they were only able to close their eyes in the darkness, and some could not even do that.

Harold wished with all of his being that he was fully recovered; if so he would be more than happy to suggest that the Battle of Hastings be decided by single combat between him and William, for this time when he spun behind William as he had done twice before he would not smash his helmet with his broadsword (he had made the unfortunate discovery that William's head was made of stone); but he would cut both legs out from underneath him with a low right-to-left slash. He was sure that he could take William in single combat next time with the new strategy, but at this point he was far from being back to normal, so single combat was not a viable option – unless it were a joust!

He could defeat William in a joust, he was sure of it. As Harold lay staring up at the stars and thinking of these matters he heard the creatures of the night calling from the heavily wooded nearby forest, and it reminded him of his sweet youth, when he and his friends only pretended to be at war with each other, and they would laugh the night away until finally the adult world called them to their homes; and they complained all the way there that this was not the way that life should be; and they swore under their breath, saying that they could not wait to become grown so that they would no longer suffer the vile curse of being subjected to these unelected rulers who called themselves adults -- and who were never children themselves and didn't understand anything. He smiled as he thought of these things, for now he was the free adult that he always wanted to be. He wondered if it was the last time in his life that he was ever to smile over anything.

CHAPTER XXXI

The Battle of Hastings

ON THE MORNING OF OCTOBER 14, 1066 the Normans and the Anglish had formed their long battle lines and were faced off against one another. The flag of the Anglish Dragon flew on one side, and the Lion of Normandy flew on the other. At the head of each side were William and Harold, mounted on horses. Harold was flanked by Gyrth and Verser. William, flanked by General Odo and General Loutrec nodded to Harold from across the field. After a moment the two warrior kings alone trotted to the center of the field.

The Anglish Dragon   The Lion of Normandy
14 October 1066 A.D.

Jesse Lee Vint

As they faced each other neither spoke but only greeted one another with a silent nod. After an uncomfortable silence, with the armies of mainland Europe standing behind one, and the patriots of Angle Land standing behind the other, William said,

"I recognize that horse."

"I think that he recognizes you," said Harold. William dismounted and walked up to Spanish Dancer, who nudged his chest and quietly snorted. William warmed his hands on the breath that was exhaled through Dancer's nostrils and then allowed him time to use scent for further recognition before gently rubbing his nose.

"I believe you're right," said William with a smile. "I believe he remembers me." King Harold dismounted and surveyed the massive troops on both sides. William continued stroking the nose of Spanish Dancer and patting him on the neck as he spoke to Harold.

"Word has reached me, Harold, that you were considering a split rule, north and south; and if so then your people would have everything north of London; ours would have London and everything south. Is that what you were thinking?"

Harold only smiled and thought to himself, "The classic strategist!"

William continued, "Your troops are tired after Stamford Bridge, what's left of them. The soldiers that you have showed up with here today...well, they're not really soldiers, are they Harold? They're just ordinary people with good hearts, and I'm sure that these wonderful people are praying that you reach an honorable conclusion, avoiding mayhem, if possible."

Harold nodded. His voice was steady and strong. "Stamford Bridge or no Stamford Bridge -- that is always the case; we will always avoid war when possible. We are only standing here today because we have been invaded, not because we love war and mayhem."

"Then if you were to do what is best for your troops, your people and your land, then you would negotiate for a split-rule, north and south," said William.

"It would be only a matter of a few months until we would be meeting like this again, William. Let me say that if you care for your troops, as I do mine, then you will accept my challenge in the center of the field in single combat."

This offer caught William by surprise and he scanned Harold's face for humor. "You're challenging me to single combat?"

"I am."

"What means of combat?"

"Jousting!"

William laughed at this. "I would never joust with the Black Knight of Winchester. No, I think the mace should be the weapon."

Harold smiled. "I would never stake the future of the Anglish on a duel with the mace-- especially if the wielder of that mace were the Duke of Normandy."

"Then you take the broadsword, and I'll take the mace."

"We tried that, didn't we William?"

"Harold, this is a waste of time. I can't accept a challenge for single combat."

"Why not?"

"I promised someone that I would bring no harm to you, so I can't win."

Harold's countenance visibly changed. "How is my future queen?"

"She's….uh, troubled…and that is all that I am going to say on the subject." William looked away, and became concerned that his voice nearly cracked, so he took time to restore his strength, breathing in and breathing out as he watched a hawk circling high overhead.

"William, your troops can't go through us, and they can't go around us, and they can't stay here. They'll have to return to Normandy. You will always be welcome here as my father-in-law and my very good friend."

William was surprised at Harold's obstinacy considering the state of his military. He was sure that Harold would have accepted his proposal by now. After all, William had eight thousand undefeated well rested, well equipped troops standing behind him. After a weighty moment he continued:

"Not too long ago there was a foggy day on the south shore of the Thames. I could have, and maybe should have killed a man that day. Now he's put to-gether an army, and soundly defeated the legendary Haarald Hardrada. That is impressive! But my friend, to your request of returning, I will say this: We are the Norse men, we are the sons of the Vikings, we are the wolves of the sea, and we never take a step backward!"

Harold nodded, "Then fate has dealt us a profane hand, William, because if you know the ancestry of our people, then you know that our ancestry is the same as yours; we are the Anglish, the sons of Germania, we are the wolves of the mountains and the forests, and we, by God, never take a step backward!"

There was a long, tense moment between the two as they both searched desperately, yet in vain, for an answer. Finally William said,

"Then it is sealed!"

William turned and started to mount his horse, but then turned back, and this time his voice did crack.

"I prayed to God this morning that we would find an honorable way out of this, Harold."

Harold was overcome with emotion himself, and re-minded William, "Just imagine if you had brought Adelize and Matilda today--instead of soldiers. It would be a time of such joy....such happiness. Just think of it! But William my brother, you prayed to the wrong God this morning. You didn't pray to the God of joy and peace, you did what you've done since you could walk--you prayed to the God of War; and regardless of what flag flies at the end of this battle, William, you will come to realize one day in the near future that for a man who has everything that a man could ever want in this life, wanting even more will prove to be a horrible mistake!"

Both were frozen, inwardly disappointed with themselves and each other over their inability to find a peaceful solution; and both were wondering whether they should hug each other, or punch one another in the face. William mounted his horse. Harold mounted his.

William looked around while clearing his throat, and then looked Harold straight in the eye and spoke softly to him.

"Harold, it's so clear: Emma, the mother of Edward is my great aunt! I'm the blood heir! The crown is mine! We had an agreement! You're the usurper! Considering these facts, my offer for split rule north and south, and offering my daughter in marriage-- does this sound like I prayed to the God of war? May God damn you today, Harold! How generous do you want me to be?"

"It is you, William, that is standing on the soil of our beautiful country with your armies stretched across our land as far as the eye can see --- and yet you speak to me of your 'generosity'?"

It was quiet for some time. Only the shrill cry of the hawk could be heard. After a moment William said," Its goodbye, isn't it Harold?"

Harold barely moved his head when he nodded," Its goodbye, William."

Both nodded to each other and turned their horses at the same moment. The short ride back to their battle lines was the longest ride of their life.

The armies on each side, even from a great distance, knew the outcome of this historical meeting by the way William and Harold had turned their horses away from one another, and all, every last one of them, inwardly said a silent prayer.

After a few minutes; some began chanting, while others raised the flag of the Anglish Dragon, of the Lion of Normandy, or of the Christian Cross. In the rear of the troops the ominous drums of war were sounded as though it were the collective heartbeat of the ancient spirits who had arrived from their holy place and had come to offer their support on the field of battle.

Harold, speaking to Gyrth and Verser, reiterated the basic strategy of establishing a fully defensive position by forming a defense of overlapping shields and forcing the Normans soldiers to run uphill and try to break through. "If we're successful, at the end of the day it will be they who are tired, and not us," he said, and then added "Once our shield-wall frustrates the Normans, then they will rely heavily on Konan the Great and Geoffrey the Hammer to make a flanking runs---Konan on the east flank, and Geoffrey the Hammer on the west. Fortify those positions with our most valiant knights."

Verser added that should Konan or Geoffrey penetrate with flanking movements, then the Anglish should have centralized reserve knights posted in the rear to intercept in either direction at a moment's notice. Gyrth and Harold agreed.

The Lion of Normandy was living up to his name and pacing back and forth like a caged lion from his position near the base of Senlac Hill while conferring with his generals.

"This is exactly what I hoped he wouldn't do," said William. "Now we will have to try to enrage his men and lure them out from their tortoise shell defense. Get Tallefer, Cleaver of Men, who is a master of this ceremony."

Moments later William laid out the strategy to Tallefer, Cleaver of Men. "Say what you have to say, do what you have to do, but entice them, lure them, enrage them, trick them into breaking their Macedonian shield-wall. Once broken, our mounted knights will pour in, Tallefer."

As the salmon is born with a destiny, so does Tallefer, Cleaver of Men know his destiny, and today his destiny had arrived. With a full heart he nodded his understanding and trotted away, guiding his horse with his knees while juggling an axe, a broadsword, and a mace. He was without a helmet.

Much to the delight of the Normans, Tallefer galloped daringly close to the Anglish line, yelling taunts and juggling his weapons. Moments later he galloped past from the opposite direction while standing on his horse's back and thumbing his nose. The Normans applauded and cheered wildly.

"Do not let this court jester lure you from your position men," shouted Gyrth.

Harold saw the danger and sent out the command to hold fast and not break the line, no matter what. Tallefer galloped past again, this time displaying his buttocks to the Anglish line, enraging several men, who threw their spears but missed. Tallefer galloped away with a wide smile on his face while walking around on the back of his horse.

Once again Tallefer passed by, this time even closer. Several men once again threw their spears, and this time it was Harold that yelled,

"Hold to, men. He's a buffoon. Throw no more weapons."

But Tallefer again rode past, this time naked from the waist down, bent over, and displaying his buttocks to the Anglish line while singing unflattering lyrics about Sir Alfred the Great.

Harold was outraged. "By the grace of God how dare that dirty dog blacken the name of Sir Alfred. I'm challenging him to a joust." Harold started for his helmet and lance when Verser pointed to a nearby hill and said, "You won't have to, Harold, somebody else already has."

Harold turned to see the Green Knight on a distant hill. The Green Knight had signaled a challenge to Tallefer, which Tallefer joyfully accepted. In an instant Tallefer donned a helmet, picked up a lance and a shield and trotted to the center of the battlefield. The Green Knight galloped to his position opposite Tallefer, and now the both of them were in the approximate position that Harold and William had met earlier. The battle lines for both sides ran east and west, and so did the line of joust run east and west. Tallefer opted to fight without body armor, unaware of the history of the Green Knight. William yelled to Tallefer to put on body armor, but it was too late; the over-confident Tallefer had already galloped to the center of the field to face his challenger.

The Green Knight, from his starting position, saluted Harold. Verser turned to Harold and asked, "He's saluting you. Do you know him, Harold?"

Harold returned the salute and said with a smile, "Aye!"

"He's fighting with the shield of the Questing Beast," said the Varangian.

"He's a brother, Bishop."

From the center of the battlefield the signal was given. The Green Knight and the Cleaver of Men charged one another, riding upright, and then as their lances were slowly lowered while at a full gallop each leaned in and eyed the weakness in their opponent's defense while canting their shields slightly to deflect the blow of one another's lance.

The Green Knight successfully deflected the lance of Tallefer while impaling Tallefer with his own. It was gruesome! The lance had entered Tallefer's chest and exited his back. His body had slid to the fulcrum of the Green Knight, who was now face to face with Tallefer. Tallefer's horse left him, leaving Tallefer completely suspended in the air by the lance of the Green Knight. The Norman side let out a collective groan, the likes of which experienced warriors on both side had never heard before.

The Anglish cheered. The Green Knight unceremoniously dumped Tallefer at the feet of the horrified Normans. He turned and started away but was suddenly hit with an arrow, and then another, and then a black cloud of arrows took down the Green Knight. The Green Knight fell from his horse. After a moment he climbed to his knees, but a knight on horseback charged the helpless Green Knight and at full speed impaled the Green Knight with his lance from behind.

It was murder. Even the Normans did not cheer this knight, who rode with a large hammer painted on his helmet. He was known by them as Geoffrey the Hammer.

"That dirty, filthy bastard! I have to break the line, Bishop, and charge the Normans! What kind of man am I if I don't?"

"You won't have to. Here they come," said the Bishop.

The Normans, battle berserk, charged up the hill toward the Anglish line. William mounted his horse and joyfully yelled to his troops while riding up and down the line,

"By the grace of the heavens God has at long last fired the engine of war! Onward Normans!"

The north men charged up Senlac Hill screaming, "God be with us!" while the Anglish rolled large stones down the hill toward them and hurled javelins, all the time yelling "God Almighty!" After a while the Normans were forced to pull back.

Harold yelled to them, "Well done, my brothers! Hold fast with the shield wall!"

At the base of the hill William conferred with his cousin of Brittany, Konan the Great; while Geoffrey the Hammer and Xavier of the Belgi listened intently. He instructed Konan to move his Keltic lancers around their eastern flank, and instructed Xavier of the Belgi to wait until the Anglish knights in the rear move toward Konan to intercept him, and then Xavier was to encircle the western flank and engage the shield wall from the rear, opening a hole, so that the troops could pour through, and then Xavier was to defend and widen that hole until additional knights arrived.

Behind the lines of the Anglish a message was handed to Verser that stated that the Green Knight's brother Malory was "Within sight and sound of the battle with twenty Scottish lancers. Please advise!"

"God bless these men!" said Harold, but was saddened at the same time because he was sure that Malory had no knowledge of the Green Knight's death, and this evening his brother would have to be taken from the field of battle by them and put on a flaming pyre in the tradition of the north man.

Harold told the messenger to inform Malory of Scotland that help was needed on the eastern flank to counter a move by Konan of Brittany. The messenger had saluted and was galloping away when Wulfgeat of Anglia suddenly turned and pointed to William at the bottom of Senlac Hill while exclaiming with his powerful voice,

"Look Harold! It's William....my god he rides like neither man nor beast, but a supernatural demon from the depths of hell."

Harold and Wulfgeat watched from their high vantage point as William grabbed a standard in the far distance bearing the flag of the Normandy Lion from a wounded soldier on horseback; and as Wulfgeat described, William rode like a supernatural demon, carrying the flag and weaving in and out of his troops at breakneck speed. When he reached an area where his men appeared to be losing heart he skidded to a stop, planted the flag in the ground from horseback, tore his helmet from his head, and as his battle-crazed horse spun two circles he urged his troops forward with these words:

"Death is behind you if you flee, and victory before you if you advance and fight. We fight, fight, fight, and by God's grace, we shall conquer for Normandy and for God!"

The troops gathered heart as they watched the unparalleled warrior sometimes known as "The Duke", other times known as "The Normandy Lion", charge the shield wall, hurl a javelin, pivot, and race parallel to the shield wall at a full gallop, knocking down shields and crushing the heads of the Anglish with his mace.

The Normans cheered William and then yelled, "God help us!" and charged the Anglish shield wall again; but using stones, javelins, and arrows the Anglish once again repelled the attack of the Normans.

The Normans began retreating, and as they did some over-zealous Anglish soldiers, enraptured by their enemies waning heart for battle, charged forward and pursued the Normans down the hill. The line was broken. This did not escape the eye of William. William returned to the base camp and spoke with Geoffrey the Hammer.

"Did you see that, Geoffrey? There was a hole created in the shield wall!" Geoffrey nodded that he observed the same thing. William exchanged his battered helmet for another while talking to Geoffrey.

"Now take your knights and circle the west flank; Xavier of the Belgi is inexperienced and will need your support -- and at the end of the day, Geoffrey, we'll see if they still call you, "The Hammer.""

"Aye, sir!" said Geoffrey.

Geoffrey put on his white helmet with Thor's black hammer insignia on the side and moved out in the direction of the western flank.

On the eastern flank Konan's knights were at great speed encircling this area nearly unopposed; but then they stopped to listen. To them, the strangest sound imaginable was coming from behind a hill. Konan's knights stopped in wonder and listened while shrugging their shoulders. But soon marchers appeared atop the distant hill playing musical instruments known as bagpipes, which sent a shiver up the spine of the Brittany Kelts. Their Keltic cousins from the north of Hadrian's Wall always brought their bagpipes and drums with them in times of battle; and these bagpipes could be heard on a clear day for a quarter mile --and that was in a wooded area; across water they say that they could be heard for several miles.

Konan's knights were listening and theorizing as to what this could mean when Malory of Scotland appeared like a wraith with his Scottish lancers in front of the small marching band of bagpipes and drums. Konan saw that these men had their faces painted in blue, and their necks where white. They had the Keltic triskelions on their shield; Konan knew who they were – they were the Keltic tribe of the north known as the Picts – and these Highlanders knew how to fight – and today these rogue Scots were fighting, not for the Anglish so much, but for the sovereignty of the island of Albion.

Malory saw Konan's troops and, turning to his own gave the order, "Lancers of Scotland, dress to the right! Position lances! Prepare for the charge! CHARGE!"

The drums and the bagpipes provided an eerie ambiance as a wave of four Scottish lancers, riding four abreast, thundered forward in perfect unison to engage Konan and his men. As they neared their opponents all lances in unison were lowered to meet the enemy. There was a loud crash as the northern Kelts engaged the southern Kelts. Malory cut loose with another wave of Scottish lancers, and then another, and another. Soon all Scottish lancers had engaged Konan's Kelts and those that were not unhorsed were fighting with mace or ball-and-chain, while many of those still on their feet were fighting with sword and shield.

From the top of Senlac Hill King Harold observed the knight with the white helmet and the hammer insignia leading a squadron of knights toward the western flank; he was sent by William to support the novice, Xavier of the Belgi. King Harold recognized The Hammer immediately as the craven evil-doer that in the most cowardly fashion one could possibly imagine murdered the Green Knight.

Harold's blood raced! It was too good to be true! He quickly located a black helmet and chain mail, confiscated it from one of his knights, donned it, and tore away on Spanish Dancer to intercept Geoffrey the Hammer.

At the foot of Senlac Hill William rode like a devil. He skidded his lathered horse into a Norman camp to exchange horses. He tossed yet another battered helmet to the blacksmith who in return pitched him a new one. A squire jogged over leading a fine destrier that had been held in secret reserve on a dragon boat and had not been ridden all day.

"Perfect!" said William, " and now I need two squadrons of knights hidden in those ravines – and I need them now!" In seconds he mounted the fresh horse and galloped away with his mace high in the air.

Harold arrived on the western flank just in time to see Geoffrey the Hammer and two of his men running down several of the Anglish who were on foot and spearing them in the back. After a moment Geoffrey looked up and froze in position.

It was the Black Knight, mounted on the huge Adalusian, who stood pawing the ground some forty yards away. The Black Knight removed his helmet and spoke to The Hammer:

"I am here, you craven miscreant, to avenge the death of the honorable Green Knight. Do you accept my challenge?"

Geoffrey observed the knight up and down, and was secretly hoping that this was not who he thought it was, for if it was then he was probably no match – and maybe he should reconsider and flee back to the Norman lines. With all of the trepidation that was presently swirling inside Geoffrey the Hammer, the fact was that his lifetime had been spent training as a knight, and now that training demanded that all doubt and weakness be pushed aside; so it was that The Hammer stood front and center, ready to meet the challenge of the Black Knight.

"Who might you be, good sir?" asked The Hammer.

Geoffrey the Hammer

"I am only a traveler who has come from the hot burning sands of hell to bring you the news of your death, good sir," answered the Black Knight.

"Does the traveler have a name?"

"I am the brother of the Green Knight."

"Your challenge is joyfully accepted, Black Knight, but before I kill you, please tell me your hidden name so that when I wear your skull on my belt and show it to my children's children, it will have a name for them to play with, along with your hairless skull."

The two knights that were standing next to Geoffrey threw back their heads and laughed at Geoffrey's fireside tavern wit. They had not stopped laughing when Harold said,

"Have it your way! My name is Harold, King of the Anglish, and I hereby grant you permission to carry the knowledge of my name with you to the afterlife. Are you ready, good sir?"

A chill went up the spine of Geoffrey. "I am ready, Black Knight," said The Hammer as he donned his helmet. Both knights closed their helmet-visors and charged one another without hesitation. The Black Knight easily deflected the lance of Geoffrey and impaled him with his own lance. When Geoffrey hit the ground at full speed he cart-wheeled with Harold's lance bobbing up and down inside of him.

Harold pulled his sword from his sheath, snapped a sharp turn, and then began trotting toward the two remaining knights, who already had their swords drawn and held high overhead in an aggressive manner; but both had a sudden change of heart; they slapped their war horses on the rear with the flat of their swords and ran for their lives.

They were, however, no match for Spanish Dancer who came up from behind them so fast that the two unlucky knights' heads, severed from their body while at a full gallop by the Black Knight, seemed to be still screaming as they flew through the air, hit the ground, and rolled like two perfectly round pumpkins through the knee-high grass.

But then Harold was knocked to the ground by an unknown assailant who had ridden up from behind.

After a brief moment of laying on his back his eyes finally focused to find a sword at his throat; now Harold could see that the wielder of that sword was none other than the Lion of Normandy, who was leaning down from his horse and staring at Harold. William's eyes looked like two burning coals in his head. After a moment William sheathed his sword, and without saying a word galloped away. Harold, whose vision was still blurred, stood and leaned against Spanish Dancer. He grabbed a stirrup for support.

Odin in the sky

As he looked in the direction of battle he saw the swirling of black and white clouds; a huge wraith was beginning to form into a giant figure taller than his palace in London; It was the figure of the one-eyed Odin, hovering over the battlefield.

Harold pulled himself up on Spanish Dancer, and when he looked a second time the wraith had vaporized and had left a twisting trail of black and white clouds.

William had returned to the front and was riding like a devil on his fresh destrier, yelling to his officers as he rode past, "Now the feigned retreat...the feigned retreat...the feigned retreat..."

The Norman troops once again charged up Senlac Hill and attacked the Anglish shield wall; but this time things were different. They feigned a retreat; some

Norman soldiers were screaming and throwing down their weapons while fleeing and shrieking in terror. Others tumbled down the hill head over heel, appearing helpless and defeated, and even crying out like small babies. It proved to be irresistible to some of the Anglish, many of them novices who were young and inexperienced, and who had replaced the warriors lost at Stamford Bridge. The neophytes leaped with joy as they pursued them down the great hill; but then William gave a hand signal and out of two ravines came a dark and terrible storm in the form of William's elite hand-picked corps of knights, who had been crouching low and waiting ever so patiently for this golden moment.

The Norman knights, like a cloud of bats that suddenly burst from a cavern like black devils at twilight, charged the novices and cracked their young bewildered skulls with the mace as they sped past and rode right into the gaping hole where Norman mace mixed it up with Anglish battle axe; and now the bloodiest segment of the Battle of Hastings was fully inaugurated, which gave Sen Lac Hill, (literally "Blood Lake Hill") its name.

For every Norman knight that fell, he was replaced by two more, until they had secured a position that made it possible for troops to ride directly to the position unscathed. A panic swept across the Anglish, and some broke the line of defense in other areas to defend the broken line. The Macedonian overlapping shield defense was beginning to crumble.

Harold, sword drawn, rode into the thick of battle near the center of the line where the Normans had created a hole. Harold dropped one Norman knight after another, and there he saw Verser the Varangian, whose terrible temperament from his dark past had returned; and swinging his battle axe with both hands had cleaned a path through the Norman knights, breaking the legs of their horses and then smashing the knight's skulls before they could hit the ground.

Harold saw the meaning of the word "berserker" for the first time since he had seen Hardrada himself fighting at Stamford Bridge as he was surrounded by ten of the Anglish. Harold's friend, 'the bishop' had left the field, and in his place stood a fully deranged madman with the strength of a Hercules that was howling like a terrible north wind. Even Gyrth stood back and eyed this man with disbelief, but soon returned to the business of driving the Norman knights through the hole and back down the hill.

After a time the hole was closed and stability to the Anglish line returned. The Normans regrouped at the bottom of the hill to evaluate what had happened. William received word that Konan and his Kelts had been neutralized by several rogue Scottish Lancers on the eastern flank, and that Konan had been taken to a dragon boat; he was barely alive, they said.

William was then told of Geoffrey the Hammer's demise, which he already knew about, and the novice Xavier of the Belgi was nowhere to be found, they said.

It was also reported that the numbers of William's elite corps had been greatly reduced by a single Herculean unidentified warrior who looked like somebody's grandfather. This baffled everyone; perhaps it was the first time in the history of the Norman people that no one had an opinion.

William's men were still reporting the deaths of several of their best fighting men as he leaned over and blew the blood out of each nostril and then wiped the blood from his eyes so that he could see. He listened to them name the names as he wrapped a horse hide strip around his right arm and pulled it tight to stop the bleeding. After Loutrec and the others had gravely informed William of the knights of the elite corps that had lost their life, William had a single question:

"Were their wounds in the front, or in the back?"

Loutrec looked at the others and then answered as William wet a cloth in a bowl of water and wiped blood from his arms and face.

"All of their wounds were in the front, William," answered the general.

"Then I'll see them in Valhalla!" said William.

Odo was sure that his brother had lost his mind. Odo suggested that during this temporary lull in the fighting that cool temperaments must reign, and that discussing a new strategy was entirely in order. "William, we can't outflank them, and we can't break their line. Why don't we try to negotiate something?"

William was handed new shoulder armor, which he examined before trying on while speaking with Odo.

"Negotiate what, Odo?"

"How about safe passage?"

This suggestion got his attention. William turned to Odo, and without rancor, as though he were asking for a glass of wild berry wine, said "Odo, get off the battlefield!"

Odo's right eye began to blink uncontrollably. He was embarrassed by this, so he gave it a mild swat to put the twitch to rest, but it persisted anyway.

"I said get off the battlefield, Odo! Do it now!"

"But where am I going to go?" asked Odo, while cupping his right hand over his troubled eye.

"I don't care if you hide in a boat, but get out of my sight."

Odo pretended to be deeply hurt by this, but after less than twenty steps in the direction of the boat he was secretly relieved, because he was already thinking of a hidden stash of meats cut in tiny squares, with bread sticks, and a small container of wine that had an aroma to die for; he had carefully rolled up these items in a piece of cloth and put them in a secret hole below the lucky number seven oarlock on The Mora during the voyage to the island.

William turned the bowl of water upside down on the top of his head and allowed the remaining cool water to splash across his face and neck before giving the order, "Loutrec, assemble the archers!"

"They have archers, too," reminded Loutrec.

"Yes, they do have archers, but they don't have bows made by Fletcher."

William chastised himself for not doing this earlier in the day, but he never imagined that Harold's ragtag Anglish would in a thousand years put up the kind of defense that he had seen today. He was sure that they would have thrown down their weapons by now, and he was greatly astonished that they had put up such a fight, considering that their resources had been greatly diminished by the horrific battle of Stamford Bridge.

William quietly admitted to himself that if Harold had not fought Hardrada and eight thousand Vikings, and had not marched from London to York and then from York all the way to Hastings, William most likely would have suffered the first defeat of his life and probably would have been killed –- exactly like the legendary Haarald Hardrada. Yes, it could have just as easily been him instead of Hardrada.

He recalled his meeting with Tostig, and felt very fortunate that his suggestion to Tostig, which at the time came as an afterthought, had resulted in the depleting and exhausting of Harold's troops prior to the battle of Hastings. At the time that he had made this suggestion to Tostig, he had no idea how absolutely golden it was. He thanked God, St. Valery, Odin, and a few others before returning to the business of fletcherizing the attack on the Anglish.

In the Anglish camp there was, like a hive of bees, a bevy of medics that had surrounded the Varangian. His left arm from the elbow had been severed. He was on his back, while the stub was pointed skyward so that the blood would not run out in copious amounts any more than it already had. Horsehide was abundant since there were dead horses everywhere; some of the hide had been cut into strips and had been tightly wrapped around his left bicep, and that had put an end to most of the bleeding. He was wide awake and cogent, though his entire body was trembling and shaking.

The Varangian demanded to know if the flanks were still protected, and by who, and if the Normans were still in a line, or regrouping, and how many hours of sunlight were left, and most importantly, were the ravenous birds of the land hovering on the Norman side, or the Anglish side – a very important sign that no experienced field general could possibly ignore;

but Harold leaned in and said, "Enough, bishop! Close your eyes and rest! We have it from here. The Normans have been taught a lesson, so our hero can now rest." The Varangian nodded weakly, closed his eyes and immediately fell into something of a coma.

During this small break many of the women and young men were quickly gathering weapons from the fallen soldiers and stacking them within the shield wall near the Anglish line so that their men would have a cache of stored weapons of every kind readily available to them when the battle resumed.

The Norman square riggers that had transported the hundreds and hundreds of bows were moved closer to the base of Senlac Hill and promptly unloaded. Archers lined up and all received their fletcherized long bows and arrows; each archer evaluated the luck of the draw and tested his bow for strength; and his arrows were examined for weight, balance, length and above all else whether or not an arrow was "true", meaning "straight as any arrow could possibly be".

Fletcher, operating as field commander, rode up and down the Norman line of archers with Loutrec at the base of Senlac hill. A second line soon fell into place, and then a third and a fourth.

The Anglish watched with a mixture of curiosity and concern, most believing the archers to be severely out of range and wondering what kind of field maneuver it was that they were witnessing.

But then and odd thing happened; the first tier of archers moved a quarter of the way up Senlac Hill, which put their archers in range, but instead of firing at the shield wall, they were instructed to aim for the area directly behind, where thousands stood unprotected. William had seen that since Harold's line was immovable and completely rigid -- by his mandate; he decided that he would have that very strategy work against him by placing his archers within a lethal distance – but still far enough away from the shield wall that Harold's men could not break the line and pursue them. If the line were broken then the archers were instructed to, in unison, send a cloud of arrows toward the vulnerable area.

Harold was notified of the garrison of archers that had suddenly, in a matter of a minutes, moved up the hill from the base. He stepped out of the pavilion where Verser was being tended to and saw that the report was true and that lines of archers had moved up from the base of the hill. These long lines of archers all had bows that were presumably the innovative composite design of longbow by Fletcher.

Harold's heart accelerated. He knew exactly what he was looking at.

"Gyrth, order the men to press close to the shields, and we'll have to move the horses back – and put on your helmet, Gyrth, and instruct all others to do the same!"

Gyrth yelled the command to move the horses to the rear which was repeated down the line by the captains. Harold mounted his horse and raced up and down the shield wall telling all to "Take cover, take cover, take cover, and don your helmets, and move the horses far to the rear!"

William gave the hand signal and a black cloud of arrows flew high in the air and over the shield wall. The distance amazed even the Norman archers, who had never witnessed such a thing. This was followed by a cloud of arrows from the second tier – and then a third wave of arrows blackened the sky. Within a short while all behind the Anglish lines was pandemonium. There didn't seem to be a safe haven. The arrows rained through the pavilions, through the trees, and in some cases through the armor and the shields of the soldiers.

Harold turned to see several soldiers screaming and running toward Gyrth, who had been hit several times with arrows and had fallen to the ground.

Harold raced toward Gyrth, and was dismounting when he was hit in the right eye with an arrow. Harold fell back against Dancer and collapsed to the ground.

With the speed of a diving falcon word traveled within the Anglish troops that King Harold had been killed on the field of battle. Within minutes many of the Anglish, who had fought so heroically, lost their will to fight – yet many fought on, saying that it was a good day to die.

This was particularly true of the HouseCarls, who fought on for God and country; and they also knew that their lives would never be spared by the Normans, who saw the Anglish HouseCarls as an elite force that would forever be loyal to King Harold and the Anglish long after his death.

From his mount, surrounded by standard bearers flying the Lion of Normandy, William yelled to his troops, "By God they are in retreat! Knights, mount your horses! Charge the line, men! Archers, do not relent! Rain them with the arrows of Normandy!" William kicked his horse into a full gallop and rode straight up "Blood Lake Hill".

The Norman knights rushed in, and after a fierce battle, finally overwhelmed through sheer numbers the sublimely heroic HouseCarls -- who had formed a ring around Harold and had fought valiantly to the last man.

The rest of the Anglish either surrendered or were killed; very few escaped the Norman storm. The Battle of Hastings had taken an abrupt turn and in a short while was effectively over.

A Norman soldier moved in and had drawn his knife and was preparing to provide some entertainment for his fellow soldiers by mutilating the last Anglo Saxon king known as Harold II when,

CRASH!

A blow from William's mace flew the soldier through the air; he landed some distance away in a tangled heap with a broken neck. The other soldiers gasped and took a step back. William turned his horse and galloped back to the deceased Harold and while pointing in the direction of a large elm tree told those present to move Harold's body and place it in the shade beneath the tree.

He instructed them to remove the arrow from Harold's eye and hand it to him when they were finished. William did not watch this procedure, but instead turned his back from it and busied himself with the matters of conquest while speaking in low tones with his generals about the coming years.

The battle had ended, he said, and now another very difficult battle was to begin; the Anglo-Saxon people were not going to roll over and celebrate William's coronation. He knew this.

When Harold had told him before the battle that his people never took a step backward, he had meant it, and they were going to, as an Anglish man would say a thousand years later during another great war,

"We will fight on the seas and oceans, we will fight on the beaches, we will fight in the fields and in the streets, and we will fight in the hills, but we will never surrender."

This meant that William would have to call in his construction engineers and start building castles throughout the land to discourage Anglo-Saxon uprisings, which could go on for centuries -- until the Germanic tribes known as the Norseman, Angle, Saxon, and Dane became a single family that spoke a single language on the new Scandinavian island that would come to be known as "English". The generals nodded their understanding.

After a minute one of the soldiers approached William with the arrow that came from Harold's eye. William instructed Fletcher to string the bloody arrow and fire it in a northerly direction – towards London. Fletcher pulled back the bow to the arrow's final length, which was half the length of the six foot bow. The arrow was released and all watched as it flew nearly two hundred and fifty yards before landing near a grove of elm and ash trees.

William's men had crowded around their hero and were waiting for him to say something brilliant about the conquest, and perhaps even congratulate them, but he simply said,

"Where the arrow has landed there will be built on that spot the finest Abbey in the land – and it will be built in Harold Godwinson's honor. It is to be called "Battle Abbey."

They all noted his request, and then watched as he walked over to where Harold's body lay still. Before he sat down he motioned the crowd away, for the exception of several guards that stood some distance from him, affording him a measure of privacy.

The battle had been won, and now William sank to a sitting position under the great elm next to the body of Harold, who he could finally bring himself to look at. There was a large pool of blood on his right eye that no longer flowed. Harold's utter stillness seemed incomprehensible to William. He leaned his back against the elm and after a moment said,

"Harold, my friend of friends, please…from your place…ask Adelize to forgive me…in the same way that you have already forgiven me, dauntless knight."

After a moment William placed his right hand on the still warm forehead of Harold, and as he touched Harold's bloodied brow there was a small electrical surge within William that released a rapid avalanche of stored memories that flashed through his mind, heart and soul with great speed for a period of time. Some of them had to do with Harold in Normandy, others had to do with Adelize and St. Valery, and those images were sometimes mixed together and were in some cases inseparable. Still others had to do with the beautiful and agonizing Matilda. These images had tunneled into his innermost being and threatened to disrupt his ability to process information accurately, generating a fear within William that he was dangerously close to losing his mind.

Beneath the great elm he leaned forward and placed his forehead on his knees; he spent the rest of his life analyzing that unique experience without ever arriving at a firm conclusion. Throughout his lifetime he would be tormented at random by an overwhelming flood of these images that were released without cause or provocation, but none compared to the electrifying moment that had occurred when he had placed his hand on the brow of his brother, King Harold II.

In time he had Harold's body moved a short distance to Waltham Abbey, where his body was entombed. It was Harold's mother that had made the request, stating that it was Harold's personal foundation and cause that had created and built the abbey, so it was only appropriate.

October 14th *of 1066 a.d.* had been a long and interesting day. The comet that Europeans had watched earlier in that year (now known as "Halley's") as it burned across the night sky had prophesied to many a great war; and this prophesy had been interpreted as "The trail of "Winged Victory" by some, and "The Devil's fiery path" by others, depending on which side of the channel they were standing on.

On December 25th 1066 William the Conqueror was crowned King of England. The Archbishop of Canterbury performed the ceremony at Westminster Abbey. After the ceremony King William turned to the large crowd and held the royal scepter high above his head; the same royal scepter that Harold had held on January 6th nearly a year earlier. Those in attendance cried out, "Long live the King! Long Live the King!"

William the Conqueror, undefeated in battle, ruled England as William I until his death twenty years later at age sixty in 1087. Matilda had passed away four years before William.

On the 15th of October 1066, one day following the death of Harold II, Adelize joined a convent and became a nun of St. Léger at Préaux in northern France, and true to her word she never saw her father again.

CHAPTER XXXII

The Wonderful Ghosts

of Waltham Abbey

Several days after the burial of William the Conqueror in 1087 the island had a visitor. A carriage driven by a very old and elegant man with tails and wearing a fashionable hat approached Waltham Abbey in Winchester.

Waltham Abbey of Winchester

The carriage came to a stop and the attendant climbed down and opened the carriage door. He assisted the passenger as she stepped to the ground. The passenger glanced in all directions, absorbing the beauty of the well-tended grounds, and then the she fastened her attention on the majesty of the abbey itself. She was a nun. After a lengthy moment of absorbing the ambience of the place she walked to the front and entered. Once inside she gazed admirably at the soaring vault of the apse, and from there she walked somewhat reverently down the aisle until the aisle came to an end. She stood quietly for several minutes before finally kneeling in front of a tomb. The nun gently placed her hand on the tomb which bore the inscription:

HAROLD KING OF ENGLAND 1066 OBVT

She bowed her head and stayed in that position without moving for a very long time. This did not go unnoticed by an unseen observer in the rear of the abbey. He was the caretaker, and he had marked the extreme devotion of the visitor.

Although the caretaker had not seen the face of the nun, he had a suspicion as to her identity. After a while the nun crossed herself, rose to her feet, and then walked toward the entrance that she had come in a moment before; but then she suddenly weaved, caught herself on a pew, and then fainted to the floor. In an instant the caretaker was at her side. After a moment she sat up, shook her head, and allowed the caretaker to help her to her feet. Slightly embarrassed, she nodded her gratitude to the caretaker and walked to the open front door to the waiting carriage.

The caretaker, still inside, bent down and picked up an object. He quickly ran out the door and caught up with the coach as it was leaving; yelling to the driver to please stop. The curious driver reined in his horses and the caretaker then informed the nun that she had dropped something. He asked for the nun's forgiveness, and then handed her the object. She smiled gratefully to the caretaker and nodded to him, while wiping several tears from her eyes.

The caretaker then produced one of his own and told the nun, "It's just like mine, Sister." He showed it to her. It was a pendant that bore the sign of the Questing Beast. She stared at it for a moment and then with all of her being examined the man's face. He smiled and said, "Come with me, Sister! Please come with me!"

Intrigued, she climbed out of the coach and walked with the caretaker down an idyllic path a hundred yards from Waltham Abbey. After a moment they reached a spot in a shaded area where there were three graves marked by wooden crosses. Carved in the three wooden crosses were the names:

BICHIP VERSER   GREN NICHT   GYRTH

After the nun had looked at the names for a minute, she bent down and picked some wildflowers.

"Like those? They say that it was Harold himself that planted those."

After a moment he asked her if he would like to know the name of the wildflower. She shook her head no, and looked at the ground while twirling the wildflower under her nose.

"And here's something else, Sister. It's what I really wanted to show you.....come over here...follow me." The caretaker beckoned her once again down an idyllic path. She followed him to a large clearing in the woods. He pointed, "Over there, Sister!"

In the corner of a large fenced area stood an old horse in his mid-to late twenties; the horse stood by himself, apart from the others. For the first time that day the caretaker saw the Sister smile. This was followed by a short laugh, and then suddenly she became quite youthful, squeezing between the two split log rails that formed the fence and stepping inside. She stood facing the black Andalusian with the single white sock, who was at least thirty yards away from her. After a moment she called to him, "Spanish Dancer."

Spanish Dancer

The old warhorse perked his head up, snorted, and continued chewing for some time while looking at her with his ears pricked forward. After carefully evaluating her, Spanish Dancer walked toward Adelize. The caretaker continued talking to her as the Andalusian approached her.

"It was the horse of our late King Harold, Sister. I take care of him. He's mine now.... and he knows you...I can see that....and so do I, know you. I know you too, Sister. I know who you are."

She hid her tears from this man while she stroked the nose of Spanish Dancer and patted him on the neck.

"And who are you, sir?"

"One of those three graves that you saw is empty. Guess which one!"

Adelize thought for a moment before saying, "Bishop Verser?"

"Just Verser now, Adelize. The Normans think I was killed--just badly wounded. It was your father who, in secret, restored my health and allowed me to live out my years as caretaker in this wonderful place."

Adelize turned to look at Verser with her blue green eyes and tear-stained cheeks. In spite of the deep agony that she had suffered for the last twenty years, she was still beautiful at thirty-eight. She told Verser that she knew of him, and that Harold spoke fondly of him many times, and then she added, "You were Harold's best friend."

But Verser instantly disputed that, saying "No Sister, you were Harold's best friend!" Adelize nearly lost emotional control, but regained it while patting the neck of the Andalusian once again.

After a quiet moment Verser asked, "Mind if I show you around, Sister? There are lots of wonderful ghosts on this land – ghosts that are still loyal to our King Harold.

Verser took the reins of Spanish Dancer and wrapped them around the bicep of his severed left arm and with his right hand he picked up a masterfully carved walking stick that was leaning against the fence rails. The three of them begin walking down an idyllic path toward a small stream, and in the distance he could be heard saying to her, "I sometimes wonder what my life would have been like if---" A moment went by and Adelize finished his thought, "If there had been no south wind."

He stopped and turned to her. She smiled. Verser returned the smile and said, "If there had been no south wind, what would our lives have been like, Princess Adelize?" This was a troubling question for the both of them. It's one that Adelize had asked herself forty times a day for the last twenty years.

Over the shoulder of Adelize, Verser saw the driver of the carriage standing some distance away through the trees with a quizzical look on his face and perhaps wondering about the safety of his passenger. Verser asked Adelize's permission to invite the man to join them. "A lovely idea!" she said, and so Verser waved his hand and beckoned the old man to join them in their walk through the beautiful wooded area. The old man happily assented, immediately ducking under branches and coming toward them with a wide smile, and even grabbing a makeshift walking stick along the way.

The four of them (including Dancer) spent the rest of the day walking the paths together while the man once known as Verser the Varangian of Byzantine gave them a guided tour and spoke freely of the friendly ghosts that had defected the Battle Abbey on top of Blood Lake Hill, and had found an inner peace in the land and the structures known to them as Waltham Abbey, the final resting place of their dauntless knight, King Harold II. It was a good day!

The End

CPSIA information can be obtained at www.ICGtesting.com
Printed in the USA
LVOW11s1917130116

470476LV00003B/76/P